Rainbows in Religions

ALAGERSAMY SAKTHIVEL

Translated by SARAVANAN KARMEGAM

INDIA • SINGAPORE • MALAYSIA

ISBN
Paperback 979-8-89588-993-0
Hardcase 979-8-89610-689-0

To

My dear wife who never ceases to be my mother with her assuring words,

My daughter and my grandsons who keep me in eternal happiness being a strong bridge between I and my wife,

My mother who fed us first even by going hungry herself when we weren't sure from where our next meal would come,

My friend Devendran alias Maaveeran, Kutti - my bosom friend, my tutor, my soul mate who keeps me happy with his songs of love when I am enervated,

All the transgender people and same sex couples who live their lives anonymously in every corner of Tamil Nadu

and

Sathya Saibaba who I hold in my heart every day.

***

Contents

Foreword

Wonders beyond repugnance

Land is considered a woman and rain, a man. As long as earth and land were common to all humans, sexual intercourse, sexuality, chastity and masturbation were neither considered sacred nor anything of one's privacy. They were seen relegated only to a level of some sexual acts performed in one's privacy. In the beginning of fifteenth century the European countries witnessed the decline of socialist values which resulted in shifting of private ownership of lands into the hands of Christian priests. Prior to this, these priests were living full-fledged family life with their women and had children too. But the ruling royalty did not like the lands of his kingdom being broken into pieces in the names of priests' heirs. The priests whose primary duty was to preach the tenets of religion were subjected to lead a life without family. Body is just a ball of flesh very often commanded by mind. When mind steps into flouting the principles of religion and trying to hide its transgressions, it becomes a private affair.

Man is a creation who falls in love with his own self and image. Here, creation doesn't mean God's creation. It is an evolutionary process. Desire in men is another form of hunger. Man has evolved through self-gratification. Self- gratification does not speak about only masturbation, an act that gives sexual pleasure. This gratification starts since the day he is an infant. Defecation is the first act of self-gratification. Anything that leaves the human body gives it happiness.

When the human mind which could fall in love with oneself and image, can fall in love with the same sex, say, a man falling for another man and a woman falling for another woman, which is not essentially against the innate desire of one's body. It is this query that had poked its nose into questioning the practicality of man-man relationship and woman-woman relationship and successfully rendered these relationships impractical, and treated the pleasure derived out of it a sin, a crime and eventually ended up with portraying it in bad light that it is something despicable. It, then, finally ended up in intervening in one's happiness. The voice of protest against this intervention rose from both men and women but remained a mute voice for long. It was only the third gender who had brought this struggle to the fore ever since the time same sex relations were considered taboo and disgraceful.

A question thus arises here: If the human race had truly treated same sex relations a repugnant one, all the literary works, anecdotes and visual media that talked about same sex relations should have perished without any taker. Shouldn't it? But the reality is just opposite to it. Amidst the great lineage of literature that normally celebrates conventional relationship between man and woman, He and She, Hero and heroine and God and Goddess, literature recently written about same sex relations is gaining momentum and occupying an irrefutable place in our literary milieu.

If any question is raised why these types of literary works should be recognised at all, counter questions in similar vein are also being asked who they are to recognise or refute it.

These feisty counter questions were not raised by same sex couples; rather these questions, louder and in singular voice, were actually raised by the third gender.

The relationship among them is not only about satiating one's carnal impulses. There is love and loyalty in it. Anyone who gets into sexual relations with a transgender would never search for a woman to satiate the demand of his body in the absence of his partner. He just waits for his partner, no matter how many more years it takes. One of these three short novels, 'The Love that Starved itself to Death' raises this pertinent query and asks whether such waiting and loyalty are found only in conventional relationship between a man and a woman.

The basis of this short novel is found in the poem *Annaseval*! *Annaseval!*, a *Purananuru* poem written by poet Pisiranthaiyar to his friend Kopperum Cholan, a Chola king. "The Love that Starved itself to Death" is a tale informing us that the fasting of Kopperum Cholan until his death waiting for his friend Pisiranthaiyar was not only about their intimate friendship but also about an invisible man-man sexual relationship found in their friendship.

The loyalty, waiting and longing for one's love in these stories leave a reader awestruck. The sudden turning points and unexpected endings change the way of enjoying its narrative style and offer some solemn minutes to wonder who could have written this story. It is none other than Alagarsamy Sakthivel.

In the short novel "La Ilaha" (literally means 'There is no God'), the story of Sarmad Kashani who is beheaded for being a homosexual, goes to Jumma Masjid with his severed head and starts singing *Kalimas* waiting for his partner, talks about the religious politics around homosexuality during the reign of Mughal emperor Aurangzeb. This short novel questions the religious tenets that exercise its control over human body and its emotions. It further places the men who claim themselves as the sole representatives of God under critical scrutiny and renders their claim absurd.

Next story, "Lunar Dynasty" gives an account of Sudyumna, the son of Manu, born as a woman, later cursed into a man and then changed into a woman and a man again and gives birth to a child. This story talks about the time of Manu. On the tenth month, when Sudyumna is undergoing severe labour pain, he changes himself into a woman called Ila and gives birth to a baby. If he doesn't become a woman, it would be a hard fantasy to think about a man giving birth to a baby. This fantasy gives way to reignite our thought on *Varnashram* and the children born out of forehead, shoulders, thighs and feet. In such cases, a question arises: who is the God of creation Brahma then and who is his partner?

These three short novels navigate different spaces of three religions. At one point it talks about the mingling of religions on the banks of river Indus after invasions from outside and how they got solidified, later diluted and finally disappeared after their assimilation with Hindustan. The river Indus never allowed any religion to stay with it long. It would just permit a religion to perish in the vortex of time if it breached the basic tenets of humanity. These descriptions about the river Indus are neither overtly a fantasy nor some cooked up narratives.

The author plays a central narrator in all these three novels and tells these stories with his profound experiences.

It is human tendency to correlate the portrayals in these stories with the personal experiences of the author. It is despicable. The author who appears in these novels travels both in the past and future. These three stories deal with the central theme that transgender is not a disgraceful clan in the society and at the same time not glorifying their births either.

Sudyumna, the son of Manu, the first ever king of human race, is portrayed as a trans-woman in "Lunar Dynasty". It has been possible in the literary imagination. We are able to enjoy that story without subjecting it to our faculty of discernment. But is it possible to have such a thing for transgender in a democratic country like ours? Are there any such possibilities opened up anywhere in this world? If these questions are raised in the minds of readers after reading these stories, we can safely assume that trans-women are not something of a third gender; rather they are our brethren.

Though the central theme, homosexuality which these three novels deal with, is not something unheard of in the world literature, they are relatively new to the Tamil literary milieu. Wonders and repugnance are not in one's birth. They are in our minds. All the wonders of this world were initially looked down upon as despicable ones. These stories written by Singapore based writer Alagarsamy Sakthivel are such wonders that lie beyond repugnance. My best wishes for him.

Andanur Su.Ra.

***

Introduction

My humble obeisance to God almighty. He is my Lord Ram. He is my Allah. He is my Jesus Christ. He is my lord Buddha. He is my Shirdi Saibaba. He is my Sathya Saibaba.

Love is something which both men and women love to have in their life. Our Tamil society and our culture, since time immemorial, had prescribed some guidelines for love. Any literature ever written, if they do not comply with the said stipulations set by our ancestors, are normally abhorred and rejected by the Tamil society.

This book of mine is one such attempt which does not comply with those stipulations of love. If we examine it deeply, we can understand it is lust behind love is the main reason for such abhorrence. Our Tamil culture tries to distinguish two types of lust- lust that can be discussed openly in public as it is perceived to be natural and lust that shouldn't be discussed in public as it is perceived to be sickening. It blindly rejects certain types of sexual relations repulsive and unacceptable. The love stories in this book seek to examine those stuff in broader perspective as to what men and women of our Tamil society normally reject as 'repulsive'.

It has been long ago since India recognised third gender. Though India removed the oppressive Section 377-A of the Indian Penal Code long ago, which earlier criminalised same sex relationship, it is true that majority of Indian men and women still find it difficult to accept sexual activities of third gender whole heartedly. One of the main reasons for such discomfort about the sexual relations among third gender is its implicit perception in the minds of people. For instance, oral sex among men and women is very common in their bedroom though it is not discussed in public. On the other hand, the same oral sex is intensely looked down upon when it comes to transgender because of the perception that they like only oral sex type of deviant sexual behaviour.

Be it a relationship between man and woman, or man and man or woman and woman, the science has never ceased teaching us that any such physical relationship which doesn't adhere to the rule of having one single partner, i.e one man to one woman, one man to one man and one woman to one woman, is always susceptible to be unsafe.

This book on third gender is an attempt to remove the so-called 'repulsiveness' towards perceived deviant sexual behaviour between men and women and change the deep-rooted, old-fashioned attitude of Tamil culture towards it by way of telling stories that it is as much as a sacred space in one's privacy.

History gets apparently very important as it becomes necessary to inform the society a good number of things from the past, from the history so as to nurture an inclusive understanding and confidence among the present generation. If we do a scrutiny on the Sangam literature of Tamils, ancient historical documents and Puranic epic stories, we find the history of India's third gender is not well documented and found only in some patchy references here and there as insignificant historical anecdotes. It is an extremely painful fact that the history of third gender has been almost hidden from the main stream by way of relegating it to some unwanted, repugnant pieces of references.

So, it becomes an important responsibility to keep the present generation informed of the history of third gender with the help of negligible number of historical evidences we have in our hand. This book of three love stories dealing with same sex relationship is an attempt in this direction. It has been written with the help of such patchy references infused with creative licence of the author.

I don't despise religions but I have been very much angry with the codes they employ to ill-treat third gender. This book is never an attempt to be critical of any religious beliefs other than discussing the ways the third gender is treated in the name of religion. On the contrary, this book talks about the core truth in all religions and respects its value in human life. I respect all religions alike- be it Hinduism, Islam, Christianity or Buddhism.

In one of the short novels in this book, I have spoken about nakedness. As though there are various view points on nudity in spiritual discourse floating around, I have taken only those references which are necessary for the purpose of story-telling. Nudity in public space is something highly debatable and this book doesn't endorse it.

It was only with the help of a weekly magazine called 'Thinnai', I could hone my skills as a writer. I sincerely thank the editor of Thinnai magazine for encouraging me with his unbroken support by publishing more than hundred stories in it.

I sincerely request all my readers irrespective of their gender, be it man or woman or transgender, to extend their generous support to this book that pledges love is sacred, blind and doesn't have gender.

Thank you.

Alagarsamy Sakthivel

Singapore

Translator's Note

Though India long ago removed its repressive section of 377-A of Indian Penal Code (IPC) which criminalised same sex relations, it hasn't left any conspicuous positive impact on the minds of people. Same sex relationship is still looked down upon as something unacceptable in one's public life and is not widely accepted as another form of sexual orientation.

Homosexuality in general and Indian context in particular must be understood in perspective. What do the LGBTQ+ communities strive for? Is it legal sanction by the government to live together? Or is it a legal sanction to marry to live in a family set up? Though India has removed article 377- A by way of decriminalising homosexuality, it is largely silent on another pestering demand from LGBTQ+ communities, i.e legalization of same sex marriage. In other words, though same sex relationship is not a crime in India, Indian courts are still unable to come to a consensus to legalise same sex marriage.

Being a conservative country in outlook, Indian psyche is still not comfortable with the notion of homosexuality due to the following factors. Firstly, Indian society considers marriage as a sacred institution which permits only sexual relationship between a man and a woman. It is believed that changing this definition would result in undermining traditional values on which the sacred institution of marriage is built. Since the primary function of marriage between a man and a woman is to procreate, Indian society views same sex relations as something unnecessary and unwanted.

Secondly, over all upbringing of children is not possible with two same sex couple even if they opt to adopt a baby. It is believed that children raised by same sex couple are more prone to emotional and behavioural problems. Thirdly, if this phenomenon called same sex relationship is unleashed, it is feared that the entire edifice of India's cultural and traditional value system would collapse and lead to other forms of unconventional relationship. India believes that same sex relationship is not 'Indian' rather it is a western concept bereft of family values. Lastly, it is believed that majority of India's population is not in favour of same sex relationship and any effort towards legalising same sex relationship or marriage will go against the will of majority of population which might lead to anarchic social systems.

Considering the above broader aspects that stand as obstacles towards full-fledged LGBTQ+ rights, it is extremely pertinent to understand this complicated issue in perspective. Barring some people who are essentially bisexual but use same sex relations to vent out their sexual frustrations due to unavailability of conventional opposite sexual partners, LGBTQ+ people are largely born as one. Just like a man or a woman who are meant to love opposite sex, they are also born with a sexual orientation meant to love same sex. Finding fault with their sexual orientation in fact points at violating one's fundamental human right to live with dignity and happiness. The broader apprehensions mentioned above are just majority opinions based on ill-conceived reality of LGBTQ+ communities. Demand of legal sanction to LGBTQ+ rights such as legalising same sex relationship and same sex marriage is not built on the basis of claiming equal rights available to conventional relationship and marriage between a man and a woman. Rather, it is based on principles of basic human rights to lead a dignified life in the society. Being a homosexual or lesbian or transgender is not one's choice he or she willingly opting for; it is their life; it is how they are born. Any demand of legalising same sex relationship should be understood on this premise.

This book is an English translation of Alagarsamy Sakthivel's Tamil book *"Aanavirkum Aanaavirkum Kadhal"* which explores same sex relationship in three different religious landscapes. The author has selected three different geographical regions for this narrative with historical and *puranic* evidences to drive home a point that same sex relationship is not a western concept as many think. It is very much *Indian*, he says. The first story which speaks about a homosexual relation between a land lord and his male friend occurs in southern Tamil Nadu. This story is written with a reference from the Tamil Sangam classic, *Purananuru* in which a king is perceived to have such an intimate relationship, a platonic intimacy, with his poet friend though they hadn't met each other till their death. Second story which speaks about intimate relationship between a Sufi saint Sarmad Kashani and his disciple Abhay Chand has its historical references in Mughal era. This story takes place during the reign of Mughal emperor Aurangazeb. The third story takes place somewhere in North India. This story speaks about a king who is cursed to become a man and a woman every month by Lord Shiva. How the things take shape after this curse does constitute the rest of the story. All these stories are desperate to bring the readers an important message: Same sex is not loathsome. It is love that drives that relationship. It is not a western idea; it is very much Indian. Existence of same sex relationship in India is a reality. Any reality which plays an irrefutable role of existence in a society must not be marginalised, and demeaned. A loud and clear message.

I sincerely thank Mr Alagarsamy Sakthivel, an active member of LGBTQ+ community for giving this opportunity to translate his book into English for reaching wider audience beyond Tamil borders and his support with timely clarifications for successfully completing this translation.

Saravanan Karmegam

Mysore

Karnataka, India.

1

The Love that Starved itself to Death

Bishop Daniel- Dindigul

O! Heart!

Read the psalms

that speak about the immortal love of my lord for me

And hail it! O! heart! hail it"

The choir standing on a corner of the cathedral was rendering this choral song composed in *Kambodhi Raga and Adhi thala* so passionately. I, the chief priest of the church, was also singing zealously along with them watching the assembly. Everyone in the crowd was singing aloud according to the cadence of choir.

I looked at left of the assembly where men were standing. I could understand that a good number of men had come to attend the prayer that day. Slowly I turned my attention towards the crowd of women standing on my left. All the rows of benches on women side were found filled with people. I was surprised to see a bench occupied only by three women. I could figure out the reason behind it.

In that row, a trans-woman Rosie Chandran was singing, sitting in the middle of the bench and two women were standing afar at its corners. Rosie, visibly undeterred by her surrounding, was completely involved in singing songs in praise of lord.

Those two women standing on both sides of the bench, without paying attention to the choir, were curiously glancing at Rosie as if she were an object of some archaic value. *'O! Lord! Forgive those two women'* I mumbled and resumed my singing.

The devotional songs sung by the choir were now over. I started conducting the day's assembly of the church. The crowd that was standing a while ago occupied their respective seats. I had already requested Arch Bishop James Ponnusamy to address the day's church gathering. Bishop James started his lecture.

"O! God almighty! You be with us! You conduct this lecture through me. My humble prayers. My lord. Amen" Bishop James prayed to God almighty and began his address.

"All of you may please turn to Galatians Chapter three, Psalm twenty-eight"- the assembly obeyed his sonorous command and started flipping the pages of the Bible to go to Galatians.

Amidst the coarse sound of papers being flipped, Bishop James recited loudly the chapter three, Psalm twenty-eight.

"There is no longer Jew or Greek, there is no longer slave or free, there is no longer male or female; for all of you are one in Jesus Christ"

"Everyone knows the meaning of this psalm. Don't you?". We are all equal before God. We are all one in Jesus Christ. There is no distinction of male, female and transgender before Jesus Christ. So, you must learn to respect everyone as your fellow being"

Bishop James continued his speech, making it lively with examples from life. I was watching James' speech with a smile.

'How come the priest talks about trans-women in today's assembly? There must be a reason behind it. Mustn't it?'- I could see some people in the crowd watching me and Rosie Chandran alternately and whispering to each other. I neglected their suspicious looks and started concentrating on the conduct of church assembly.

The prayer had just been over. I was standing at the entrance through which the people would exit. Most of the people who came of out of the hall greeted me. Only some of them threw a demeaning glance at me and sneered. I just ignored their condescending chuckles.

Everyone left the cathedral except me. Bishop James, his wife and his daughter left for their home nearby. I strode slowly to my house. Rosie Chandran was eagerly waiting for me there. "What stew should I make today, father? Chicken or mutton?" her guileless voice woke me up, I looked up to her face and smiled at her.

"Rosie, whatever you make with your expert hands, it will be tasty for sure. Do make whatever you like" Rosie grinned at my reply.

Her smile didn't bring the same on my face, rather the mindset of this society about her, in fact, pained me. I went inside the room and reclined on the sofa.

My mind was full of thoughts about Rosie Chandran. *'Rosie is a very beautiful girl. She sings very well. Good hearted girl. If everything in this world is due to God's mercy, her birth as a trans-woman is also due to His mercy. Isn't it? Why does this society refuse to accept this?'*

I felt my head aching.

Bharathidasan Chinnappan- Rasakkapatti

"There is one Pisiraanthai,

The one who thinks of me as his soul.

Though he might not come to meet me when I am rich,

He would surely come to me

When I am in trouble"

– Purananuru (215)

Sitting in my tile-roofed home lying at the Esanatham-Pallapatti Road, I was reading *Purananuru.* It was raining heavily out there. I was reading the book enjoying the sound of rain incessantly hitting the tiles above. My bare chest, in its attempt to adjust with the chillness of sudden rain, grew warmer. I closed the book and delved into deep thoughts fully occupied by Kopperum Cholan and Pisirathaiyar.

These two men, Kopperum Cholan and Pisiranthiayar are not new to me. However, I always had some apprehensions about their friendship. Ever since the college days during my undergraduate degree, I have been arguing on this matter with my friends.

"Two men who never met before sacrificing their lives may be a theme of fantasy in present day politics and movies. Some fool from somewhere may self-immolate himself for a politician whom he had never met. An idiot may commit suicide grieving the death of his favourite cine-star. But Pisiranthai was not a fool. He was an erudite poet. Kopperum

Cholan was also not an idiot. He was the king of a state. Their friendship that had blossomed without meeting each other and ended in their death must have some unfathomable secret in it. Who knows?" – While murmuring myself, Aranmaniyar's domestic help came to meet me.

"Ayya, Aranmanaiyar is extremely sick. He asked me to bring you immediately." He said. I put on my shirt and went down.

In order to avoid delay by taking detour in the usual track, the bullock cart driver took a short route and drove the cart faster. All the villages around my place were arid lands, we would get rain only occasionally. That too, as this was the first bout of rain in this season, the whiff of red soil, which was otherwise extremely hotter due to scorching sun, rose from the ground and pierced my nostrils.

Seemai karuvelam trees were found thickly grown along the cart track running into the wild. As I was sitting on the hoodless cart, the thorny branches of those trees occasionally hit my face and hurt it whenever the cart was shaken while speeding on the uneven beaten track. Amidst this agony, recurrent appearance of Aranmaniyar kept coming over my mind.

It was said that all the villages around my place were well rain fed and fertile. But today, all those villages had become near barren lands due to lack of rain. If there had been one good man who was still celebrated with high regard in all those villages, it was our Aranmanaiyar. He would be present in almost all the functions held in villages, be it heading the village Panjayat, temple festival, rooster fights, chicken pox prevention camps, taming bulls or even funeral.

Rasakkapatti is not my native town. Kurumbapatti, a village in the cluster of those eight villages around, is my birth place. It was Maruthappa Nayakkar, the father of Aranmanaiyar, who got this slum boy educated. Veerappa Nayakkar, known as Aranmanaiyar today, is the son of Maruthappa Nayakkar.

While Veerappa Nayakkar was born in palace and I was born in a slum. Yet we both studied in the same school. It didn't matter what the villagers spoke of us, my friendship with Veerappa Nayakkar was beyond our castes. It was a very thick friendship. I am presently working as Tamil teacher in the school run by Aranmanaiyar in Rasakkapatti. I am the only privileged person who knows about the personal life of Aranmanaiyar.

Veerappa Nayakkar had only one male heir and is now living alone in his palace after anointing his grown up, married son to look after his wealth. He is living in a house far away from his palace along with two servants and a cook. I am still unable to comprehend why he had chosen such a life of loneliness.

I reached his home. I strode away fast to the room where Aranmaniyar was lying down. Lying on his side looking towards window, he heard the sound of my footsteps, and kept grumbling about something without turning his face to me. I went near to his cot. He didn't seem to recognise my presence.

"Chandran…O! my Chandran. My dearest Chandran..." he kept moaning the name Chandran without even being aware of saliva drooling at the corner of his mouth.

“I am Bharathi…Aranmanai….Aranmanai” I shook his body anxiously. Only after this, he could understand that I had come.

“Bharathi…Bharathi…” he held my palms into his and cried like a baby. I didn’t understand anything why he was crying. Without uttering anything, I just paid attention how to assuage his woes.

“Aranmani…who’s that Chandran?” I asked him calmly.

Aranmanai cried violently as his lips were quivering. “Chandran is my uncle’s son. He is my life. O my dear Chandran! I don’t know where he is now. I will die only after seeing my Chandran”- I was left stunned at his violent cry and aggressive laments.

We had discussed hidden secrets of Aranmaiyar’s life on many occasions but he never told me anything about Chandran.

‘Who’s that Chandran?’ I grew perplexed.

Bishop Daniel- Dindigul

I met this trans-woman Rosie Chandran six months ago. The cathedral in which I had been an Arch Bishop was located in the middle of Dindigul City. There was a big school near the city bus stand and the cathedral was on the school premises. The residential quarters of pastors working there were very near to the church. I was over all in charge of the Christian monastery which enjoyed all these facilities in one compound.

In our monastery, the pastors didn’t have to remain bachelors like those who work in Roman Catholic Church. If a pastor wants to marry, he could very well marry and get children. I didn't marry. I lived alone. Rosie had just come to my home. I could eat tasty meals nowadays only because of Rosie's culinary skills. It is Rosie who is now looking after most of my personal works.

...

One day midnight six months ago, I heard someone yelling helplessly by the road that ran near my residence. I woke up. I could vividly hear someone imploring loudly "Please leave me...Please leave me". When I heard some men threatening her in intimidating tone "Come with me now. Don't act chaste woman" I became alert.

I sped to the main gate of the church. The watchman Xavier was sitting on a stool on the corner of the gate and was literally sleeping. "Xavier...someone is struggling for life and howling for help. Don't you hear that? Hell with your sleep" I reproached the watchman.

"No father...." He fumbled something in half sleep. I sent him to the place from where the sound was coming. Xavier quickly left and returned with Rosie Chandran.

On seeing her, I couldn't understand she was a trans-woman. I asked her, "Who are you child?"

"My name is Rosie Chandran, father" she replied. Her reply revealed that she was a trans-woman.

"Where are you from? Why do you travel alone in this midnight?" the words were hardly out of my mouth, she burst into tears and sobbed inconsolably. She explained everything.

Her real name was Chandran. After becoming a trans-woman, she changed her name as Rosie Chandran. Being an orphan, she had come to Dindigul in search of livelihood. A man who was lusting after her had insisted her to have sex with him. It was at that time Rosie, as she was intimidated, screamed.

I felt pity for Rosie. "O.K. I will offer you a place to sleep tonight. You may leave tomorrow morning" I said.

I got a house on the other side of the church cleaned by the watchman and made her stay that night.

When I was getting ready for the Church works next day morning, Rosie Chandran came to me. I thought she had come to say good bye. But she didn't come for that.

"Father, I am an orphan. Please offer me a job here. I can cook well. Please give me a job and a place to stay" her words in tears softened my heart.

'She is also a creation of Jesus Christ. If a person like me who serves God does dislike her, who else would support her?', I thought.

I thought she must be about thirty years old seeing her youthful appearance. When she told me that she had already crossed forty-five years, I was surprised.

"Other than cooking, what else do you know?" I asked her.

"I was working in an Iyer's home before this. I learnt music there, father. So, I can teach music to a couple of interested people, father". Her reply brought me a smile, I laughed.

"In church too, we used to have Carnatic music concerts. But you need to learn those songs. It may take some time. First you cook for me. Is that O.K?"

Rosie bobbed her head enthusiastically. I wanted to know about her knowledge in music.

'Everyone thinks that Carnatic Music is thriving only in Hindu temples. It is wrong. The songs sung in Churches like ours, are mostly based on ragas and Talas of Carnatic music. When I was studying in monastery's theological school, I also learnt music. It could be one of the reasons why I liked Rosie much.' I looked at Rosie.

'It is dangerous to keep her stay overnight like this. If any untoward incident happens, I will only be responsible for it.' So, I decided to keep her at my home and took her there.

Very soon, Rosie had learnt to maintain the household works efficiently. I was surprised at her smartness and sharp intellect.

One day I asked her to sing a song. Without any hesitation, she started singing a song heartily. Her voice did lack softness but was full of feminine grace. Her sweet music sung in unwavering pitch got my heart softened. I also accompanied her and sang some Christian songs composed in Carnatic music.

Very shortly, Rosie Chandran could successfully master all the songs sung in the Church. In addition to it, when she proved her prowess in western music, I openly appreciated her in front of everyone. But those 'others' had different eyes, and were still suspicious about me.

While I was relishing the delicious meals made by Rosie daily, the people who came to the Church, on other hand, were busy gossiping about our relationship and spitting out scandals about us.

Not giving a damn to the scandalous opinions about us, I just resumed my usual service to God leaving those scandals to the mercy of Jesus Christ.

Bharathidasan Chinnappan- Rasakkapatti

Aranamaniyar was not even sensitive to his running nose; nor willing to wipe off his drooling saliva. I felt pity for Aranmanaiyar seeing him whimper.

'He lived a life that everyone envied. He had property that no one had ever dreamt of! But he is now living alone like an orphan. Why doesn't he like to live with his son? Who's that Chandran?' I summoned up my courage and asked Aranamanaiyar about it.

The reply he gave me amidst his uncontrollable sobs left me terribly shocked.

He told that Chandran was his male lover. Male lover for a man! What sort of a disgust is this? I thought of spitting on his face on hearing it. Bur Aranmanai was my childhood friend; my bosom friend. So, I must not behave in a way that could potentially make him feel insulted. I had a hard time to swallow my spittle.

Aranamanai was not in a condition to feel my disgust. He seemed to have been so determined that he wanted to speak out everything lying in his heart that was never shared with anyone till now. Severely gasping for breath, Aranmanaiyar stuttered when narrated his story.

"Bharathi, this society may not accept a man falling in love with another man. But I am one of those men who dared this society and lived with a man after falling in love with him. Chandran is my uncle's son. Younger to me by four years. You are my close friend only in school. Once I came out of school, Chandran was my closest pal. The desire that dictated our youth had brought us together and united us in sexual relationship. There was hardly any day left in the palace we hadn't hugged each other and slept in the room given to me" Aranmanaiyar was relaxed now. But my sense of disgust on him didn't leave me yet. Aranmanaiyar resumed talking:

"Bharathi, I am not ashamed of telling this. I had never even thought that I would marry a girl and get children one day. This thought had never occurred in mind in my youth. But Chandran was my lover during those day when I wasn't married. He was my wife…He was everything to me…our happiest, beautiful life was disrupted by a quake- like incident one day. My father saw us kissing each other. Chandran bore the brunt of his anger. He was beaten mercilessly. It was when he ran out of the palace not to return anymore. He didn't return after that incident"

I felt as if I was listening to a filthy story. His words made me laugh.

"But…Aranmanai, you don't look a woman. Do you? We have been watching your masculine prowess in *Silambam* and *Rekhla races* held in all eight villages around here. It is very hard to think of a man like you having this dark side of desire."

Aranmanaiyar threw an innocent look at me, looking up to my face.

"My dear friend, without judging me please do consider my precarious situation and feelings…show me some mercy, my friend", I saw his face imploring me.

"Bharathi, it is true that I was a brave man. But courage and lust are no way related to each other. Chandran was not like me. He was profoundly feminine. I never wanted to justify my love for him just because of it. I simply liked the infatuation between man and man. It is the truth. I am a villager. I am not all that educated to give an intellectual interpretation of love between man and man. I need my Chandran now. That is all I want. You can only bring him back to me" he grasped my hands tightly with his, overwhelmed with emotions.

"Bharathi, I beg you holding your hands as your legs… please…"

I couldn't stand his pain anymore. "Enough Aranmanai… it's enough" I cried. The misery of my friend Aranmanai was now flowing down as tears from my eyes.

"Dear friend, don't worry. It is my duty to find out Chandran and bring him to you"

I wiped his running nose and drooling mouth with a piece of cloth and caressed his head for long. He fell into sleep.

…

I came home. When I entered my home after washing off my feet, I saw the book Purananuru. 'Poet *Pisirathaiyar could have been like Chandran. Was it because of this his friendship with King Kopperum Cholan hadn't been known to anyone?* I was completely confused with unanswerable questions. However, I was very firm in one thing- I must find out Chandran, no matter what it costs. I have to produce him before Aramanaiyar.

I was getting ready for sleep.

Bishop Daniel- Dindigul

"Our humblest regards to

Jesus Christ, the benefactor

The lord of three worlds.

The shiniest soul on this planet

The lord with golden celestial feet

The lord of wisdom

The lord of omniscient music"

On that day, I could hear large number of people in the church singing this song composed in *Surutti* Raga and *Adi Thala* in chorus. The piano music that accompanied the song softly touched the heart.

As Bishop of the church, I just completed the Morning Prayer and was enjoying my leisure at home. There were a lot of men and women assembled in the church to partake in choir on account of Christmas festival. I was taking notes from the Bible for the evening lecture.

"Father", Jenifer came running to me, whining. '*If Jenifer comes to my home searching for me, there must a serious problem in the church that can't be solved easily*'

"What Jenifer! Anything serious? Is anyone creating problem?"

"It is Rosie Chandran, father" when she gave this reply, I became alert. '*Rosie is not sort of a woman who creates nuisance*' thinking of Rosie, I walked to the Church along with Jenifer.

David Sagayam was filling the entire church with the usual sweetness of his piano music. Men were standing on one side of piano and women were on the other holding their song books. Rosie Chandran was standing alone in a corner without mingling with anyone. I could understand the problem.

'Rosie is a trans-woman. Her voice is masculine. So, I wouldn't be able to include Rosie in women's group. At the same time, asking Rosie to sing along with men would amount to insulting her femininity. What to do?' I could understand that others were also undergoing similar predicament.

This predicament got me amused as I had to find a solution to this issue.

"Rosie...please come here...This song has been composed in *Surutti* Raga in praise of Jesus Christ. So please sing a prelude in Surutti Raga...it would just be enough if you could sing a prelude with the basic sa..ri..ga..ma..pa.. tha...nee swaras"

Rosie could understand my intention. She thought for a second, and started humming a prelude. O! God! She sang that prelude containing some intricate niceties of music!

"Rosie, your prelude is simply fantastic. Just pay attention to your pitch while singing and keep it high. It will enhance its quality". Her prelude came out with more finesse.

I didn't stop nagging her. "Rosie, try changing your voice and simply hum the prelude without deviating pitch". Rosie did exactly what I said.

I sang Rosie's third prelude in western music. Rosie could grasp its essence beautifully. Now three preludes were ready.

I led Rosie to the spot where piano was being played. I placed her, to stand alone, among men and women.

“David, please start the piano music for this song. David began playing it. When David’s piano stopped playing music, I asked Rosie to sing the first prelude starting with *sa-ri-ga-ma-pa-tha-ni.*

Rosie started singing in her mellifluous voice. Sooner she completed singing I asked ‘*Tabla*’ Robert to play *Tabla* separately. Once Tabla playing was over, I asked both men and women singers to sing their part. Both men and women performed their best that day. Robert played his *tabla* according to their modulations. It was just wonderful… wonderful. *Pallavi* and *anupallavi* were over now.

Next, first *Saranam* was to be sung. Just like the *pallavi* sung initially, David’s piano did its work first followed by Rosie’s humming of prelude, *Tabla* accompanying with its solo play, and men and women singers singing along with it.

Now, subsequent *saranams* were to be sung in sequence. Rosie infused western music while singing her preludes in all those *saranams.* It was just a blissful moment! The voice of singers along with piano music took the entire song to different level of bliss.

I asked the entire choir once again to sing the songs the way I taught them. This time the music and song were better than before.

Everyone’s face carried a sort of tranquil and happiness. Rosie’s face was brightened up with delight. It was evident that everyone liked Rosie seeing her singing, standing more prominently among them with her silvery voice. Not only on that day, when she sang songs standing in the middle of choir many liked her singing. Many people evinced interest to know her back ground- who Rosie Chandran was and where she was hailing from.

Along with it grew some scandalous rumours about the relationship I shared with Rosie. I grew bit worried when I understood that those rumours were strong.

Bharathidasan Chinnappan- Rasakkapatti

It had been nearly one month since I promised Aranmanaiyar to find out Chandran and bring him back to him. During the last one month, all my sincere efforts to search for him in every village around went in vain but I still continued my efforts without losing hope.

In my last attempt, I could taste some success. I was informed by a man that Chandran was frequently seen roaming with a *'Pondugan'* namely Kumar living in Esanatham. Next day, I was in Esanatham. I could easily find out *pondugan* eunuch Kumar's house.

The men who walked like women, talked like women, and behaved like women were addressed with a nick name '*pondugan*'. When I saw Kumar being addressed with that name, I could easily understand how Kumar would behave.

Kumar didn't come to the place where I was sitting. Kumar's elder sister only received me. "Both Kumar and Chandran wanted to become women. Kumar used to tell everyone that he wanted to go to Chennai for that. One day both of them were missing from Esanatham" she said. I was hugely disappointed to hear his elder sister hissing this matter into my ears.

"Our distant relative Kuppanna is living in Chennai near Saidapet railway station. I think they might have gone to his house. This village is teasing Kumar and calls him 'pondugan'. We also thought it was good not to call him back to our village" Kumar's elder sister paused her talk.

I went to Chennai in search of Kuppanna. I travelled in an electric train from Chennai Egmore to Saidapet. *'I have to find out Kuppanna in that huge crowd of people. Would I be able to do that?'*

I approached some elder men chitchatting at a tea shop near the railway station exit gate and asked them hesitantly, "Does anyone know Kuppanna here?"

"Kuppanna or Kuppamma?" one of them asked me this question sarcastically. Others joined him and laughed hysterically. I couldn't get why they laughed like that.

"Hey…lad!" He called out to a boy, told him, "Take him to our '*Ajakku*' Kuppamma". Others sitting around him laughed again. I didn't understand what he meant by '*ajakku*'. Only after meeting Kuppanna, I could understand what it meant.

He was wearing a lungi joined in both ends, a kurta on top usually worn by women and a thin cloth wrapped on his chest to display that he was a woman. He looked more than sixty years old. His beard wasn't shaven for days. Kuppanna was standing in front of me not as a man; and not as a woman either.

"I am coming from Kurumbapatti near Pallapatti" I told him as I cleared my throat. Hearing my words, his face became bright, came near to me and glanced at my face calmly. When he said that he was also hailing from Kurumbapatti, I was shocked.

"Is it? Whose house are you from?" I asked him in haste.

"I am from Ramar Ayya's house. Yours?" These words from Kuppanna made me restless. *'Kuppanna is also from my slum area'*. My eyes welled up with tears seeing his deplorable condition. "Why did you come here leaving your home?" I asked him.

"You have seen my condition yourself now. How can I live in that village Thambi? You must be ten years younger to me. All you might know for your age would be only about caste problem. At your age, you mightn't have known how our own men of our village went after eunuchs like me to get rid of us from the village. Where else can piece of a shit like me go other than this Chennai city? "Kuppamma heaved a sigh.

I remained silent. Kuppamma made a tea for me. After having tea, I was relaxed.

"Did Kumar and Chandran come here?" I touched on the subject directly.

Kuppamma smiled. "Why are you asking me to talk about a story which took place twenty years ago?" *she* told.

I didn't tell her anything about Aranmanaiyar. "Nothing important. Both are from our village. That is why I am interested to know" I told her in a lowered voice.

"Both of them came here, Thambi. They wanted to change themselves as women. But, alas! How would I narrate what had happened that time?" Seeing her hesitating to tell me something about them, I encouraged *her* to speak it out.

“In those days there were no sophisticated surgery that are available today to change one’s gender. There was an ironsmith workshop nearby. They would do something in secret in the night as they were afraid of police”

Kuppamma continued. They had a specially made blunt short iron rod in that workshop. One has to sit on its end…”

“Sitting on the tip of iron rod?” I was terribly shocked at hearing that.

“They would make the man nude who wants to become a woman and then make them sit on the iron rod’s blunt head so that it gets inserted into their anus. They would repeat this process again and again….”

I could no longer listen to her story after that. For the first time, I felt seriously pity for the transgender women. That too, Kuppamma, my own clan, caste. She had already been humiliated in the name of caste being a lower caste *man*. Along with that, she had undergone this torture too…

I was unable to control my tears from flowing down. Kuppamma continued.

“You are crying Thambi, aren’t you? People like me will have something to eat only if we *sit* like that. Men will visit us only after that. I could somehow manage my living those days only with this mouth and anus”

I came back again to Aranmanaiyar’s topic. “What did then happen to Kumar and Chandran?”

“They didn’t like this harsh method in ironsmith workshop. They were with me for some time. It was when a Hindi speaking lady came here to settle. She was a citizen of Thailand. She was running a massage parlour in Thailand.

These days even for massaging, shops have started coming up, Thambi" Kuppamma spoke innocently with her eyes wide open. I grew worried as I still couldn't trace out where Chandran was.

"So, Chandran and Kumar are not here. Are they?" I asked her softly.

"Listen to the story fully, Thambi. The Thailand Hindi lady somehow convinced those two boys and took them under her control with sweet coated talk. She convinced them saying that in Thailand, the doctor would change one's gender by surgery, there are no such facilities here in India, even if they do such surgery here, no one would respect eunuchs in India, they would ridicule calling them *ajakku, Ali* and *nine number*. But in Thailand, they are respected and eunuchs are high in demand- hearing such assuring words from that Hindi speaking lady, these two men got ready to move to Thailand. I fought with that Hindi lady but in vain. But she and those two men didn't even budge an inch. Once I fought with her telling her I would drag her to police, she got intimidated. After this fight, one day all of a sudden, all three disappeared"

I felt as if I was travelling in pitch dark. *'How am I going to trace out Chandran? How could Aranmaniyar bear this disappointment?'*

I was about to leave. Kuppamma went in, remembering something suddenly and came out with an old piece of paper.

"Thambi, one day I was venting out my anguish about the sudden disappearance of those three to the house owner of that Hindi speaking lady. The house owner lady gave me an old paper and told that she had given Hindi lady this house for rent on the basis of this passport copy. This paper may be useful for you. Take it"

I snatched that near moth-eaten paper from her hands. It was a copy of Thailand Passport. It had the Hindi lady's complete Thailand address printed in it.

I went back to my village holding the address in hand and disappointment in heart.

Bishop Daniel- Dindigul

O! Lord of three tasks, Namaskaram.*

One of them yourself, Namaskaram

Lord of actions, Ocean of mercy

Forever omniscient, Namaskaram

The king of all worlds, Namaskaram

The creator of all beings, Namaskaram

O! Benevolent creator of

Land, sea, life, and sky, Namaskaram

**Creation, Protection and destruction*

I heard Rosie Chandran singing this song composed in *Sankarabharanam* Raga and *Adi Thala* from the backyard. That song was not new to me; it was usual one I listen to every day. But newer musical niceties that she infused in it were something amazing. Rosie was a gift of God. Lying on bed, my wavering thoughts about Rosie run amok incoherently.

I slept well today and didn't attend the church. As I was suffering from mild fever and cold, I decided to remain at home for some rest and had requested Bishop James living below my quarters to conduct the mass in the church.

I was awake, but didn't get up from the bed. I heard the same sweet song again. But this time the singer was not Rosie. It was voice of a woman. Enormously surprised, I sped to the backyard. My brother Peter and Diana were sitting along with Rosie. It was Diana who was singing now. I was surprised at their sudden visit.

"How are you, *Anna?* How are you, Diana? I greeted them both. How are you doing Diana?"

I noticed Diana. She was in full white clad. No one could tell that she was fifty. But, white sari, white blouse, white head cover…the way she looked at me with that white dress, I felt something uneasy in it. I chose to avoid direct eye contact with hers.

"I will be back in a while after bathing. You please be here" I told Diana and went to bath room. While taking bath, my mind was full of Diana.

Diana was my neighbour in Chennai. She was my close friend while studying in college. We had shared and discussed many things of our life.

Diana was madly in love with me. I was aware of it. But I never attempted to arouse her desire for me. To be very precise, I had never thought about such thing.

I joined a theological college entirely on my volition. It was only after I studied theology in depth, I could feel the magnificence of Jesus Christ getting into my heart and change the course of my life. The spiritual energy god gave me, filled in my heart in its fullest and I considered service to god the only aim of my life and began forgetting my family life.

Diana married a man and led a happy life for some time. Her marriage that started in happy note ended with divorce shortly. After that, Diana was completely involved in the service of god. I was, at times, worried about her and her present life.

After a long time since the death of my father, my brother peter had come to meet me. All of us had our meals without a word. Rosie Chandran was serving the food. Sooner the meals were over, Rosie and Diana went to the main door of the house and I retired to my bed room. Peter came behind me, and sat beside on the cot.

"Brother Daniel, I had been telling you get married since long. But you had flatly refused to listen to my words...but now, would that be right to keep a transgender woman with you?"

"Anna, what are you talking? Please don't denigrate my service to God" I fumed.

Peter didn't speak anything about it after that. But his words had been bothering me for long.

Peter and Diana left the home after sometime.

I grew angry and called Rosie Chandran.

"Rosie, where were you born as Chandran? Tell me now. I will take you to your home town to leave you there for ever"

Hardly had I spoken these words, Rosie broke down and wept uncontrollably. I understood she became angry at my words. '*Today morning I thought she was a gift from God and in the evening, I am determined to send her back home. What sort of a funny destiny is this? Why does Jesus test me like this?*'

Bharatidasan Chinnappan- Rasakkapatti

Around the Indian Hotel in Thailand, were there a lot of massage parlours. The street which was exclusively known for massaging services had a large number of Indian settlers. Both sides of the street were replete with Indian restaurants. Everywhere heard mixed sounds of *aavo…aavo*. Varieties of Indian cuisine such as *Sabji, Pulav, Chappathi, Thandoori* Chicken, *Paneer* etc were on display in the shops.

The Hindi speaking Thailand lady who had brought Kumar and Chandran was living somewhere near in this area. With the address found in the passport copy, I was trying to trace that Thailand lady's residence. But it wasn't that easy without knowing how to go about. The thought of Aranmanaiyar came over my mind.

Last month when I came to Rasakapatti from Chennai, I first went to Aranmanaiyar and showed him the worn-out copy of passport.

I tried to convince him that it was nearly impossible to trace out Chandran in Thailand and it was better of him to forget everything about Chandran and lead a normal life. But he didn't even budge an inch and was very stubborn.

He threw his eyes over that old copy of passport and felt happy as if he had met Chandran. Seeing his happiness, I couldn't help laughing but controlled it.

He took out some stacks of currency notes from the bottom of his cot and tossed them in front of me. He then raised his both palms together, joined them in utter obeisance.

"My dear friend, it is because you I am happy today. Thank you so much my dear friend. I am sure that I would meet my Chandran. I would die only after he came to me. So please do not lose faith and keep searching him in Thailand. I'll tell the accountant to get your passport ready"

It was his resolute stubbornness which had brought me to Thailand. '*This time I will return home with Chandran*' I vowed myself.

I somehow managed to find out a Tamil restaurant after a tireless roaming on the streets of Thailand. I went to a youth working over there and showed him the torn copy of passport of the Hindi speaking Thailand lady.

"Thambi, I have to go to this address" I told him.

He was happy meeting a person who could talk to him in Tamil and took me to that address.

That house, looked a palatial bungalow, had almost all its corners replete with only massage parlours. On one side, Thailand women howling "massage…massage… and on other side Indian women yelling out the same. Along with them there stood a bevy of bouncers guarding those women.

I could assess the situation there. '*The moment I drop those costly words that I have come there to take Chandran along with me, rest is assured I would be beaten black and blue*'. I was very cautious with palpitating heart.

I walked towards the Hindi speaking women walking half naked. Displaying all her teeth, one of them took me along with her to a room upstairs.

"Half hour, hundred Baht…one hour, two hundred Baht…body massage…oil massage" that Hindi lady went on listing out the rates of her services.

If only I stayed there, I would be able to find out where Chandran was. So I kept prolonging the massage. Seeing me spending more time, other women in that room chuckled at me. I didn't understand why they laughed at me but later understood that if someone took more time for massaging, it would end up in receiving 'other' pleasures as well.

From the moment she started massaging my body, I kept mumbling 'Kumar…transgender….Chandran… transgender'. Hearing my laments, they were just laughing it out in the beginning. Sooner they heard me bemoaning calling out the names Kumar…transgender and Chandran transgender, they became angry with me. I was petrified at seeing them raging with anger.

One of those women looking stout shouted something in Hindi. Next moment other women moved away from me. I didn't get what was happening. As they had already taken off my clothes, I was lying down almost naked with a small towel covering my groins.

A beautiful young lady came near to me when I was lying on bed. She massaged my body exquisitely and that special application of massage did evoke something in me. I was stunned at hearing her voice while massaging my body. Her voice was not of a woman. Her voice sounded masculine. I understood that she was a transgender. Those Hindi speaking women who heard me mumbling 'transgender' must have sent me this trans-woman.

I had never touched any transgender woman so far in my life. I had a strong dislike for them and spat out on the very sight of them earlier. But now I was lying in the hands of a transgender!

Like an expert masseur, she was kneading my body elegantly. The softness of her hands! My body seemed to be under the spell of her skilful hands.

Slowly going down, her hands were now at my groin area gently fondling my private parts. I was not in a position to stop her hands. She did all her magic there.

'Truly speaking I am not a chaste man in the matters of sex. I had brought many women to my bed and enjoyed sex with them. I belong to lower caste anyway. But in the matters of women, in villages no man would see if he belonged to lower caste or higher caste. It is still prevalent in villages where a lower caste man seduces a woman from upper caste despite knowing the fact that he would either face extremely harsh punishment or severe repercussions that include his death. So, I am not weak in the art of seduction anyway.'

This transgender woman sitting beside me was giving me '*that*' pleasure with her mouth which those village women normally refuse to give. I was often experiencing, enjoying what was called heavenly bliss with her tricks and at one point I couldn't resist myself. My body, well built with frequent intake of pearl millets, finger millets and corn, was now longing for something bigger pleasure. I gestured to her and she began taking her clothes off.

"How would she be looking after taking her clothes off?' What Saidapet Kuppamma had told about iron smith's workshop and blunt- tipped iron rod came through my mind. No matter what it was, I sensed that my body wouldn't bear the pain of longing anymore. I became ready for anything now.

She didn't look that way different I was apprehensive. She looked completely woman in her privates, may be with surgery. I was doubly happy seeing her.

I was done with everything. I gave that transgender woman money as much as I could, the money given by Aranmaniayar. She was immensely happy. I remembered Chandran again and started uttering Kumar…transgender… where are you?"

"O! You need Kumari?" when she asked me this question in Tamil, my happiness knew no limits. "Yes" I just bobbed my head like a bull. *'At last, I could find Kumar'.*

Kumar alias Kumari was in an attire like other Hindi speaking women seen downstairs. When she asked me "Who are you? What do you want?", I became visibly overwhelmed with emotions that were waiting to be discharged like flood.

I narrated the entire story that ranged from Aranmanaiyar, Chandran to everything till now in detail. She was listening to all with her eyes wide open. She found it difficult to believe that someone from her village had come that far to meet her. She could believe it true only after a long conversation.

I was patient enough and asked her where Chandra was amidst my gasping.

"Mama, we both, I and Chandran came to Thailand together. But after arriving in here, our land lady sent both of us to different places. As arranged earlier, I underwent a surgery. I believe Chandran must have undergone similar surgery too. But after that, we didn't…"

"What? What happened after that? I asked.

"I came to know only after three months that they had sent Chandran back to India. Chandran didn't agree to the terms of Madame to get into sex trade. At last, forgoing the amount she spent of him, she sent him back to India. I opted to stay back here as I could enjoy both money and sex in plenty" Kumari paused her talk a minute.

I was silent, not in a position to speak.

Not only was my body, my mind also was down with helplessness. I came back to my hotel and threw myself onto bed.

'Aranmanai....my dear friend...the luck isn't in your favour, I think. How much more I can try beyond this?'

Tears welled up in my eyes beyond my control. *'Now it is of no use staying in this country anymore. I should leave for India immediately'* I fell asleep.

Bishop Daniel- Dindigul

'Rosie Chandran is innocent. I have hurt her heart by telling her to get out of the house. While serving God in Chennai and then serving in this church in Dindigul after transfer, I have earned a reputation that Daniel is a good Bishop. It was my selfish thought, that the reputation I had earned would get spoiled by Rosie Chandran, had made me speak like that to her.'

'O! Jesus! Satan must have got into my mind. Please get me rid of him. I have rebuked an innocent soul. Pardon me for that', I beseeched Jesus Christ.

At that time, I reminded of myself that the Head Bishop from Chennai would be visiting tomorrow. We had arranged entertainment programmes on account of his visit. In one of those programmes, Rosie Chandran was to give a talk for one hour. It was going to be her first episcopal lecture. I rebuked myself for being harsh with her at this important moment in her life.

It was midnight. I noticed that Rosie Chandran has already left for bed. I went to the dining hall and saw meals kept ready there. Rosie had kept the food separately. *'What a beautiful heart is hers!'* I relished that tasty meals not whole heartedly and went to sleep.

Next day, the Head Bishop conducted the prayer himself. Other Bishops stood behind him.

After the prayer, the chief Bishop came to the dais. Since the function was presided over by the chief Bishop, the hall witnessed a huge crowd. The servants engaged to attend some specific functions of the Church were trying to control the crowd that had assembled in extraordinary numbers here and there.

All the programmes arranged on the day of Chief Bishop's visit were over one after another. I was eagerly waiting for Rosie Chandran to come up on dais to give her talk.

The scheduled time of Rosie's talk had thus arrived. Rosie went onto dais. She first offered prayer to God almighty. "The Bread of Life" was the topic of her talk.

'What a superb lecture she gave! Truly speaking, it wasn't she who had given that talk; it was God who had gone into her and delivered the talk that day'

She quoted many references on 'the Bread of life' and enthralled everyone with newer visions which no one had ever thought of. Everyone assembled there was completely amazed at her eloquence of spiritual understanding of the Bible.

Her talk sounded like magnificent water-falls flowing down from a hill top. Her songs pouring like rain resembled the coolness of water droplets from the falls that comforts one's body. The crowd that was listening to her talk was almost spell bound standing at the zenith of ecstasy. I too felt getting teary eyed. At last, Rosie had won.

Rosie completed her speech. The claps of audience filled in the hall accompanied with the huge cry of 'hallelujha'. It took nearly two hours for both sounds getting subsided. At last, the chief Bishop gave his speech. "This trans-woman, Rosie Chandran is a divine '*Yaazh*' of God almighty. Now this yaazh not only belongs to the Church in Dindigul but to all the churches throughout Tamil Nadu. The music of this Yaazh must be played in every corner of Tamil Nadu. The headquarters of our church would make all the necessary arrangements for this". Hardly these words were out of Bishop's mouth, the huge applause of hand claps tore open the sky.

Rosie's life did take a different course after that. Now Rosie Chandran was not living with me but still living in my heart. Presently she is living in Anna Nagar in Dindigul city and spreads the gospel messages all over Tamil Nadu. Where ever she went, the crowd of Christians assembled in huge numbers.

Not only Dindigul city, one could see hoardings and posters- *Our trans-lady Rosie Chandran calls you*- almost in every corner of Tamil Nadu. Apart from this, she was praised as a resurgent spiritual angel in the world of Christianity. All my achievements in the area of spirituality had now looked a tiny heap of sand before a mountain when compared it to her achievements in the field of spirituality. Yet, I was proud of her achievements.

Bharathidasan Chinnappan- Rasakkapatti

'Considering eminence a most rewarding

And friendship his life line,

My king had gone there when he was in distress.

Isn't a matter of highest praise?

If such a man says 'he'd definitely come'

His heartfelt friendship and acumen of immaculate

Personality get anyone astounded'

From the moment I boarded the flight I kept thinking of the verse 217 in Purananuru. As declared categorically by Kopperum Cholan, Pisiranthaiyar did reach him that day. Would this Chandran come like that? My thought was fully occupied with Chandran and Aranmanaiyar.

I reached Chennai airport from Thailand and took a train to reach Egmore railway station. The Superfast Express train leaving for Trichy from Egmore was scheduled to arrive in minutes.

I felt completely fatigued both physically and mentally. It appeared that I wouldn't be able to find out the *Pisiranthaiyar,* Chandran, and the dearest lover of my bosom friend *Kopperum Cholan,* Aranmaniyar.

This Kopperum Cholan alias Aranmanaiyar is extremely confident in saying that his Pisiranthaiyar alias Chandran would definitely come to meet him. But whereabouts of Pisiranthaiyar was not yet known. Would *she* one day come in front of Aranmanaiyar as a trans-woman without announcing *her* arrival? How would she look like? Would she be looking like that beautiful trans-woman with whom I had sex? I felt like laughing.

The train arrived in. I boarded the train and occupied my seat. Feeling very hungry, I bought something and ate it. The train left the station. '*What sort of a deep love is this? Let it be a love of a man with another man. For Aranmanaiyar, it would have been an easy task to get men of his choice with his money. But his love is something beyond all these. The very thought of Aranmanaiyar got me astonished and at the same time thought of it stupid too.*'

When I was in Thailand, I had to get into sexual contact with a trans-woman due to some circumstances. Her body was really beautiful and she gave me a pleasure boundlessly which other women were unwilling to give. Now all these were over. I had almost forgotten that trans- woman and began having sex with my wife after I went back to my home. Aranmanaiyar could opt such possibility of finding pleasure. Couldn't he? I felt a simultaneous surge of pity and anger filling in me while thinking of Aranmaniyar. I looked out to the window to divert my thoughts about Aranmanaiyar. My eyes fell on a big poster.

I read that poster fully carrying an advertisement in big letters "Trans-woman Rosie Chandran calling". It was a call for a Christian gospel meeting. The name of the speaker, trans-woman Rosie Chandran, had been written in big block letters. The complete address of the church, Dindigul was also found below her name.

"Trans-woman Chandran.... Trans-woman Chandran...O! God! I have finally found him. I have found Chandran. I seemed that I yelled it aloud. The passengers who were travelling with me looked at me oddly. But I was not in the position to take note of their apprehensive expressions.

I could feel a sort of ecstasy pervading my body. I sincerely prayed to god '*Please get me the glimpse of Chandran this time. I have gone through so much of failure and feel exhausted.*' I sincerely prayed to our family deity Madurai Veeran once.

The train reached Trichy station. I ran to the entrance. The ticket examiner was checking the tickets and letting the passengers to go out one by one. I ran out of patience to stand in the queue. Disregarding the abuses of people standing in front of me, I quickened my steps to the ticket examiner. As soon as I came out of the railway station, I took a taxi and left for Dindigul. It would take minimum two hours to reach Dindigul. I was praying to god all through my journey. Finally, I reached the Dindigul Church. I settled the amount with the taxi driver hurriedly.

The church gate was found closed. My good time, the watchman was sitting in front of the gate. "I have to meet the pastor. It is very urgent" I told him in an extremely anxious tone.

"Who are you?" the watchman looked at me doubtfully. I ran out of reasons and told him voluntarily, "I am relative of the pastor. In a way he is related to me as brother". The watchman asked me to wait there and went in. I stood awestruck looking at the magnificent church standing before me. The Cross fixed on its wall was throwing a gentle smile at me. I was praying to God, '*Oh my Jesus...protect me*'.

Both the pastor and the watchman came running to me fast. The pastor gazed at me intently and I saw his face disappointed seeing me. I could understand why his facial expressions got changed and I jumped in hurriedly.

"I am sorry father. I wanted to meet you. It is very urgent. It is about a person's life and death. It is only you who could save his life" I told, begged him.

"Why did you lie for that? Please come in", the pastor reproached me for lying. I didn't speak anything. The watchman opened the gate and I followed the pastor.

The pastor went in and brought me a glass of water. "Get yourself relaxed first" he said.

'*Ahh…this pastor is a good man*'- My hope grew stronger.

"I…am searching Rosie Chandran, father. My closest friend's life is hanging on the desire to meet Rosie. You must be benevolent enough to extend your help to save his life." Tears welled up in my eyes.

Listening to my words, the pastor's eyes grew inscrutably expressive. "Rosie has relatives. Hasn't she? It gets me astonished. She had told me that she is an orphan. It's alright anyway. Please tell me the whole story about her" the pastor told.

I told him every bit of truth. My story that began in Rasakkapatti, Aranmanaiyar, Chandran, the sexual intimacy between them, how Chandran had become a transgender woman, the life and death struggle of Aranmanaiyar- I didn't leave anything that I could remember.

Patiently listening to all what I told him, the pastor became teary eyed. "Jesus is greatly merciful. He is our shepherd to guide the prodigals." I was very much delighted listening to the pastor.

"Your friend will definitely get well soon. Chandran will definitely come to meet your friend. Don't worry" when he uttered these words I clasped his hands tightly.

"Thank you so much father. Thank you" I raised my hands, folded in utmost reverence struggling to utter words. *'Now my family deity Madurai Veeran is none other than this pastor'.*

The pastor was silent for some time and then spoke: "Rosie Chandran is not here. She has gone to Madurai. I will contact her in her phone and bring her there tomorrow. Now you may leave for your home. Where do I have to come tomorrow with Rosie Chandran?"

"Father, first you reach Esanatham bus stand. I will make the necessary arrangements to pick you both from the bus stand by bullock cart to Aranmanaiyar's residence" I spoke politely.

"O.K." he nodded his head, went in and came out holding a rosary with the Cross in his hands.

"Give this rosary to your friend, Aranamaiyar. This rosary would bring him good luck. Jesus will never abandon anyone. You please comfort your friend that Chandran will definitely come to meet him shortly. I will be there along with Rosie Chandran tomorrow afternoon. Is that O.K?"

I paid pastor my regards and left.

I somehow got to reach Aranmaniyar that night itself.

"Aranmani…you are a lucky man. Your soul mate Chandran is going to come here tomorrow. I explained him everything that had happened. "Is it? Is it? O! my Chandran… my Chandran" Aranamaniyar rose and managed to sit.

"The priest told that he would bring Chandran here tomorrow. Here is the rosary he gave me after getting it 'energised'. Keep this rosary on your chest. You will be alright." I spoke, nearly stammering out of overwhelming delight.

Aranmanaiyar seemed to have entered into some world of fantasy. I came out of the outer entrance and asked the watchman whether I could get *country* liquor. He scratched his scalp for a second before running somewhere. He then returned with liquor bottles. I drank it stomach full and then relished completely the meals given in palace. "I have to leave for Esanatham tomorrow morning. Get the bullock cart ready" I told the watchman and lay on my back.

Bishop Daniel: Dindigul

The story narrated by the man who had come from Esanatham got me deeply moved. I dialled Rosie Chandran's telephone number hoping to know where she was. I understood that Rosie had returned to her house at Anna Nagar in Dindigul after her lecture in Madurai.

"Rosie, you need to come with me to a place tomorrow morning. Be at your Anna Nagar residence. I'll come by taxi to pick you"

O.K father. I will be ready. Anything important?"

When Rosie asked me this question, I couldn't help narrating all what had happened. I told her everything right from the story narrated by the man from Esanatham who was searching for Chandran.

Later we both discussed the health condition of Aranmaniyar through phone. Rosie now understood the need of meeting Aranmanaiyar in person. I could understand from her words that she was very clear in her stand. I hung the phone up after a lengthy conversation with her and lay on bed. My head ached mildly.

'What would Aranmaniayar do when he meets Chandran? Would he ask him to stay with him? It isn't possible. Is it? If not, would he go to Dindigul to settle down with Chandran? What would Rosie Chandran think of Aranmanaiyar's love? What would Chandran think important- love or service to Jesus?'

It was past midnight when I could release myself from my chaotic mind.

Bharathidasan Chinnappan- Rasakkapatti

I took bath in the early morning and left Aranamaiyar's house by bullock cart. It took nearly half an hour for the cart to reach Esanatham bus stand. I didn't go anywhere from the bus stand as I was very much confident that pastor would be truthful to his words. I was keenly watching every car and bus entering the bus stand. Mind kept chanting Chandran's name. Exactly at eleven a taxi rolled its way into the bus stand. The pastor got off the car followed by a beautiful woman. I understood that it must be Rosie Chandran. Though she was aged, her body still exuded beauty and youth.

"Please come father....Please welcome...: I greeted them both and got them into the cart. The bullock cart was now marching to Aranmanaiyar's house. This time too, the cart driver drove the cart by the same short cut. The cart made unpleasant sounds as it was navigating uneven ground. On the other hand my heart was pounding with trepidation to know as to what had been destined to happen next.

I noticed both Rosie and pastor. Their faces looked as if hardened. Rosie didn't speak, looking around fixing her eyes somewhere. We reached Aranmanaiyar's house. I helped them to alight the cart and then ran into the house.

"Aranmanai....Aranmanai...Your Chandran has come to meet you. He has come Aranmanai..." I yelled out and ran in. Pastor and Rosie followed me. Aranmanai managed to get up and sat straight. My happiness knew no bounds. I gestured to Rosie Chandran to come near to Aranmanai.

"Aranmanai....look here...here stands your Chandran. Look at him. Have a look till your eyes get wet"

"Chandran...My dearest Chandran. O! My soul! How could you forget your mama my dear Chandran? How could you stay away from me these many days?"

The servants of the house came running to his room hearing his yells.

Aranmanai was sobbing inconsolably. "Why don't you come near to me my dear?" I thought Rosie would approach him lovingly hearing his sobs of desolation. But she.... she didn't even try going near to him. Instead, it was the pastor who jumped in the front and ran to him screaming "Mama...Mama". As he went near to Aranmanai, the latter cuddled him so tightly. The pastor's back arched, adjusting with Aranmanai's tight hug. Aranmanai showered kisses on pastor's face with his drooling mouth. The pastor stroked his head lovingly as his eyes welled up with tears.

I was completely stunned at seeing it. "If so, this pastor is Chandran. I went to Rosie hurriedly. I saw her crying silently. I asked her, "Rosie, what is the full name of father?"

When she told that pastor's full name was Daniel Chandran, I screamed out of control, "O! Is it?"

"Chandran…O! My Chandran! I keep going with this life just for you my dear." Aranmanai cried like a baby.

The pastor grew extremely anxious at hearing Aranmanai's rants. "Mama…I was *dead* long ago. I am now void of any personal desires. It was only after my desires were dead, I could submit my body and mind to the service of Jesus. Your Chandran is now dead mama….Now I am Daniel Chandran. Bishop Daniel Chandran mama.."

The pastor kneeled in front of Aranmanai and cried his heart out.

Aranamani smiled at him and said, "You are dead. You are dead. Aren't you? Then this body is just a skeleton anyway. My dear…now I must then die happily. I thank god for showing my Chandran when I am dying"- Aranmanai fell onto the ground unconscious as he was speaking.

I acted swiftly to grasp his hands from falling. But everything was over. Aranmanaiyar had already breathed his last. His hands were still tightly grasping his beloved Chandran. The rosary that Chandran gave him was dangling from his other hand.

We all cried. But the pastor didn't cry after that.

"Jesus is omnisciently magnificent. My mama has gone to the kingdom of God. From now on all will be at peace" the pastor spoke lucidly. He looked at me and told, "Make the arrangements for Aranmanaiyar's funeral." I bobbed my head swiftly. Hearing the news of death, Aranamaniyar's son came running there. The servants at his home were busy running here and there to look after the tasks assigned to them for funeral. I felt that it wouldn't be alright to keep Rosie and the pastor there anymore. I took them in a bullock cart and reached Esanatham.

In the bus station I picked some time to talk the pastor again. "Father, do you know what all the places I roamed searching for you? I went to Chennai…and then to Thailand."

The pastor spoke calmly. "It is all true. It was true that I went to Thailand along with Kumar. But unlike Kumar, I was not willing to sell my body, which only my mama could own, to others for giving them happiness just to earn money. I didn't undergo surgery to change my gender to become a transgender too. As I fought with the landlady in Thailand, they sent me back to India fearing police and external affairs department. After reaching Chennai, I was roaming in the streets like an orphan. A kind hearted pastor in the church found me and gave me shelter at his home. He got me educated along with his sons. After that, he understood my interest in studies and got me admitted in a theological college and made me a pastor."

"I almost forget my mama. I buried all my pains in the service I did to god as a good pastor"

The pastor completed his story. Rosie now talked. "I was shocked and astonished listening to your story you narrated yesterday night. But today, you have risen as high as sky in my heart, father".

A taxi arrived in. The pastor and Rosie boarded the taxi and left.

My heart remained heavy and felt that I needed some rest. Sooner I entered my house, I saw the copy of Purananuru.

Suddenly I was overwhelmed with an urge to cry my heart out. A while ago, I had witnessed another version of Pisiranthai's love unfolded just in front of my eyes. Aranmanaiyar died waiting for his love. *Pisiranthai* was *dead* and became a saint just to forget his love. I went to the verse 67 of Purananuru. I started reciting that verse sung by Pisiranthai longing for Kopperum Cholan, aloud, rendered it with an exquisite feeling of love.

"O! Dear swan...O! Dear swan...

In this evening

when the moon shines in its fullest

like a benevolent king's face

who guards his land beaming with pride

of winning war,

I grow gloomy

as I am unable to go to my soul mate"

I saw my wife staring at me and heard her muttering irritably "This man has gone mad...gone mad"

End

2
La Ilaha

Nude Sufi saint Sarmad Kashani, Prince Dar Shiko and disciple Abhay Chand.

Abhay Chand- Delhi- later part of seventeenth century

"My uncle

He was born as a Jew; later became a Muslim

He lived as Muslim and later became a Hindu

During his ending days as Hindu he became an atheist

My uncle became an atheist."

I was singing Hindustani ghazals, playing my Tambura "*Ektara*" thinking of my beloved uncle on the banks of chilly Yamuna River in the midnight on that full moon day. My fingers were trembling, unable to play the strings of Ektara- a quite unusual one today. Amidst my sobs, the rhythm at some places in my ghazal became irregular. My voice grew shaky with the deep sadness that had crept into my heart. Yet, I didn't stop singing thinking of my uncle.

It appeared that the Taj Mahal standing on the other side of the river shining under moon light seemed to have been watching my woes and inner conflicts with an empty look. A pitiable monument! What else could it do anyway? After all it was just a tomb where love remained buried. Just like a love that had been buried under the Taj Mahal, my homosexual love with my uncle was also buried under that graveyard lying opposite to Jumma Masjid yesterday.

The love of King Shajahan for Mumtaj had never been insulted anywhere. But the love my uncle had on me - his male partner, was literally abused by Aurangazeb, the son of King Shajahan, and got humiliated in every sense. After outraging it, our pitiable love witnessed its ignominious burial in this graveyard lying in the front. How cruel it had been!

Today morning, in the court of ruthless ruler Aurangazeb, all Ulema- the learned men had assembled.

When the quasi judge ordered my uncle in harsh tone to recite the complete Kalima Tayyab in that court where ulema men were present, I was really shaken inside. But my uncle kept on smiling even at that juncture. Everyone assembled there knew well the complete meaning of Kalima Tayyab "*La ilaha illalaaha*". It means there is no god other than Allah. When my beloved uncle kept telling the first sentence "la ilaha" which meant "There is no God" with stress, other Ulema priests assembled in the court of emperor Aurangazeb known otherwise as Alamgir, stood united and expressed their angst in unison.

"Your highness, this man Sarmad Kashani is in fact a Sufi, not a priest. He is a *kafir*, an atheist".

All those Ulema priests pleaded the emperor, "Your highness, this man Sarmad Kashani is critical of the omniscient Allah. He has been cheating the people of Delhi and you must give him a suitable punishment." Emperor Aurangazeb's face bore its usual unsympathetic expression. He didn't speak anything to ulema priests. A quasi judge sitting in the court spoke in the place of Aurangazeb.

The cold eyes of the judge fell on me who was standing at a distance, trembling.

"Drag that eunuch here" the quasi judge roared. Two guards grasped my hair tightly, dragged me along and threw me out in front of my uncle, Sarmad Kashani.

My mama was standing nude as usual. It was the divine nudity which I had been seeing for nearly twenty years. *'A large crowd of people from the city of Delhi is just waiting for him daily in front of Jumma masjid to touch and pay homage to his phallus. But these men sitting in this court see my mama's nudity obscene. As per the tenets of the Shariyat, my mama's nudity is a big crime, they say.'*

"O! The men of this court! My mama always loves Islam. Doesn't he? Don't you understand that the state of being a Sufi in Islam is a quest for Allah within oneself through meditations without searching for Him outside? Or are you all feigning ignorance despite knowing the fact about his state of an Islamic Sufi?" I cried within without venting it out.

The guard who was grasping my hair didn't leave his grip. I was watching my mama with unbearable pain in heart. Mama also glanced at me lovingly. His eyes evoked my love for him from my heart. *'My lord! I am extremely anxious at what these ruthless men in this court would do to you. You had earlier performed many miracles before your devotees. Hadn't you? Won't you perform one such miracle now in front of these courtiers?'* I wept within, silently.

"Hei…Sarmad Kashani. Who's this man Abhay Chand? Is he your male lover?" The quasi judge yelled out to my mama. My mama didn't reply to the quasi judge's question. As my mama didn't reply, the quasi judge looked at me angrily and yelled, "Whip this eunuch called Abhay Chand till his skin is peeled off. Only then his husband Kashani would speak out". Hardly his words came out of his mouth, the lashes of whip tore my skin like thunder.

But what had got me surprised was that those lashes thrown didn't hurt me even a little whereas my mama writhed in pain for every swing of whip upon me. The crowd stood spellbound watching that spiritual master perform miracle by receiving all the blows thrown at me as if they were lashed on him.

Even at this critical juncture my mama spoke without losing his composure. "Hei Quasi Judge! I always love Islam, not only today but for ever. But I would like to tell you one thing. Islam is not a collection of some laws as you think. It is a manifestation of pure love. It is not plain rules of the Shariyat"

The quasi judge yelled at him again for his reply. "Then why did you pronounce half of Kalima Tayyib "la Ilaha" and confirm that there is no god? Doesn't it mean that you are a *Kafir* who denies the existence of god?"

Mama negated the judge calmly. "Quasi Judge! I am still living with unsatisfactory impressions that what I hold on till date are just insufficient means to realise god. I am a man who is still longing to realise God. As I am still struggling with my incomplete knowledge about god, I wouldn't dare to lie 'Allah is god' who I haven't fully realised in me. On the other hand, I am unable to accept your accusation that I am a *kafir* just because of my incomplete realisation. I love Allah, not only today, but tomorrow and for ever"

The quasi judge became angry at his words. His words got harsher. "Sarmad Kashani, do not hide the truth and restrain speaking lies in this court. What did you speak about Ahmad's Meeraj pilgrimage before your devotees at Hare Bhare tomb in Jumma Masjid? Tell us the truth"

I was watching my beloved mama. The gem among the Sufis, my mama, glanced at the courtiers and spoke in a definitive affirmation. "I would now tell you all about what I spoke of Ahmed's Meeraj pilgrimage. All our Mullahs say that Ahmed went to heaven. But I, Sarmad, tell you, that it is heaven that had come to Ahmed. It is the actual sentence I spoke that day. Why should the prophet, the merciful, undertake a journey to heaven? It is the heaven that must come down in search of the prophet, the god's messenger. It is what I actually meant by that statement"

"Quasi…it's enough. Speak no more" the emperor Aurangazeb roared. The entire court fell silent.

"Quasi Judge, this foolish Sufi Sarmad Kashani has accepted his crime of having insulted the holy pilgrimage of the Prophet. So, you can pronounce the degree of punishment now" Aurangazeb ordered. The quasi-Judge obeyed his authoritative tone.

"Drag him, the Sufi Sarmad Kashani, to the Jumma Masjid. Behead him in front of the Masjid"

Mama smiled at the pronouncement of punishment. Many in the court weren't happy with the punishment and murmured, "It is unjust. Very cruel". The atrocities that followed it, the way my mama was dragged along the streets of Delhi came over my mind one after another and made me cry helplessly while standing on the banks of river Yamuna.

The frogs resting on the banks of the river were intimidated with my fiendish cry and jumped into water. I kept on weeping. It took a long time to get my tormented heart cooled down. Now the weather became chilly. The moist air of the river Yamuna caught my tender body shiver. I looked around and saw some people were burning dried twigs in fire at a distance to keep themselves warm. Carrying my 'Ektara' on my shoulder, I walked towards them. While walking I felt my feet stumbling on some dead bodies that came ashore. Among those reeking bodies, I noticed some of them lying headless.

Had it been some other day, that gory scene would have had me frightened to the core. But I saw my beloved mama's headless body yesterday. Would my fear for headless bodies have anything to do with me now? Never. Exasperated, I walked towards fire. Five or six persons were sitting in front of the huge ball of fire. Some of them were Hindu Sadhus with ash smeared on their foreheads. Others were Islamic Sufi saints. Without uttering a word, I sat by the flames. My body was still shivering due to cold.

After a brief silence, the well-built Sufi sitting beside me came near to me and looked at me intently under the light of flames. It was only when the stench of *Ganja* emitted from his smoking pipe hit my nose, I had had a good look of all those saints sitting there. Everyone had a smoking pipe in their hands. I was embarrassed at seeing them. This one, a well-built one, who was looking at me very closely stuck up his conversation with me.

"You…you were in Aurangazeb's court yesterday. Weren't you? You are that intimate lover of Sadguru Sarmad Kashani. Aren't you?". I gazed at him with embarrassment. It was no secret to see mendicants smoking *Ganja*. I could see the traces of true spirituality shining on his face through the stenches of *Ganja*. "Yes swamy…" I just bobbed my head. Other Sadhus stared at me in amazement hearing my reply.

A Hindu Sadhu spoke first. "Sarmad Kashani was a Sadguru searching for god through meditation. Nudity is a stage in Sanyasa of Hindus. It is highly improbable that the stupid brain of Aurangazeb would be able to understand what it is." Other Sadhus were silent listening to him. The he resumed his talk.

"The king Aurangazeb is just an ordinary mortal whose understanding of god is not beyond the open spaces of sky. How could a person like him appreciate someone like Sarmad Kashani who asks to search for Him, the god, within you? It is why that ruthless man killed Kashani without showing any mercy". The Hindu Sadhu's tone reflected his anger.

Another thin- bodied Sufi saint who was listening to the Hindu Sadhu intervened and spoke. "But the story I heard is different from the one you are telling now that happened yesterday. The stories I had gathered from the people of Delhi were totally different anyway"

“It is true that Aurangazeb had got Sarmad Kashani beheaded for reciting the half of Kalima Tayyib *‘La Ilaha’*”

“But I heard from the people that Sarmad Kashani carried his severed head in his hands, entered Jumma Masjid and recited the remaining half of Kalima Tayyib “*Illallaah Mohammed rasoolullaah*” aloud before disappearing into the sky. Aren’t you aware of this? Sarmad Kashani has proved that he was a true Muslim”

The Hindu Sadhu got angry at these words. “It may be true. It may be false too. But Sarmad Kashani loved Allah, Moses and Ram. That is why he was called Sadguru Sarmad Kashani. He had recited a Rubaiyat song that he had been searching for Ram and Laxman through Prophet Mohammed. You must remember all these”

Other than the well-built Sufi saint, all other saints were seriously countering each other’s views vehemently with their spiritual arguments. I remained silent. That muscular Sufi saint yelled at others. “Please don’t talk anything more. That great soul, Sarmad Kashani wasn’t a Jew, nor a Muslim, nor a Hindu. He was beyond all these and the one who reached God through the path of love. We still need time to understand his holy utterances. So, let us restrain ourselves not to argue about it.”

All Sadhus were silent. I liked that muscular Sufi monk. I leaned on his powerful shoulders and lessened my burden of sorrows. “Thank you Bhaiya…My brother” He understood my condition and comforted me.

That saint’s shoulders were as powerful and broad as my mama’s. This Sufi saint’s face was also as calm as my mama’s. Embodiment of peace. Despite my best efforts to control my emotions, I couldn't help thinking of my mama. I cried desolately thinking about him. I wet the Sufi's shoulders with my tears due to incessant sobs.

He remained quiet and kept glancing at me compassionately till I stopped crying. It seemed that he just desired to calm me down somehow with his efforts.

"Dear Brother Abhay Chand, please remember one thing. Do not think that you and Sadguru Sarmad Kashani alone were the ones who had male- male relationship in this world. We hear the famous Sufi saint Guru Rumi who introduced fabulous whirling dance form of Islamic Sufism to this world was madly in love with his male tutor. I hope you must be aware of this. May I sing a ghazal song sung by the Sufi poet Rumi to get you some relief from the pain you are undergoing now? Can you play your 'Ektara' to my song?" I said yes.

The saint stood up. Once he rose from the ground, other saints who were warming themselves on the river bank also stood up. The saint mixed up two ghazals of Rumi and sang them as one with resonant voice.

"Whenever your heart is broken, do dance

Even when all your bonds of love are torn, do dance

Amidst the feuds of cunning, do dance

Even if you see blood flowing, do dance

Light can penetrate only though bruises, and

In the bruises that give you pains, the light penetrates"

Under the inebriation of *Ganja* and glee, the Sufi saint was dancing, whirling on the sprawling river bed of Yamuna. Other saints joined him with their chorus and danced along with him. Being intoxicated with the sweetness of the song, other Hindu Sadhus also joined the dance keeping their *Ganja* smoking pipe aside. I kept on playing the strings of my 'Ektara'. After sometime, that Hindu monk picked the 'Ektara' from me and started playing a pleasing song in it. I joined those Sufi saints and began dancing.

Sufi dance is not new to me. I had had danced with my mama so many times. But today mama is not with me. I danced whirling around and around just to forget my sadness. The sadness that had been overpowering me did now start waning slowly.

As said by the Sufi poet Rumi in his Rubaiyat poem, now light had entered my aching bruises. Slowly I got rid of the darkness that had hitherto crept into my heart and saw the light of enlightenment.

Everyone was tired due to dancing. It took a lot of time for me to get tired from my whirling dance. Now other than the well-built Sufi monk and I, others were busy going back to their huts to make their beds. I was left alone with that Sufi monk.

The Sufi monk gently cuddled me and asked, "My brother, the city of Delhi is already aware of the intense love between you, Abhay Chand, and Sadguru Sarmad Kashani. Even Sufism which is very liberal in one's feeling towards god has never spoken anything against male- male sex relationship. I was able to guess what he was about to ask.

"My brother Abhay Chand, all what I ask from you is just a simple one. How could a superlative saint like Sarmad Kashani fall in love with a man like you? Under which condition he could develop such as intimacy which he could boast of having it only between him and God? Where did your same sex relationship start? Could you share those details with me, brother? I remained silent without replying to that monk's questions. I was deeply thinking about it.

In my individual capacity it was nearly impossible for me to explain him the divine relationship I shared with my mama. It was possible for my mama to express his love for me through his Rubaiyat poems for the world to feel happy about it. But would that be possible in my case? I grew anxious. On the other side, I realised that only if I could reveal our love to these enlightened saints, the legacy of our intimate love would reach the generations to come.

I prayed to my mama sincerely. "My beloved mama, would you join me now to tell about our love? Would you come over to this river bed of Yamuna for my sake?" my heart melted thinking about my mama. Suddenly I felt a fragrance which I was so much familiar with approached very near to me. It was…it was….the fragrance of my guru, my beloved Sarmad Kashani's saliva.

It was that sour stench that used to get into my nostrils when he took my lips into his, wetting it with his spittle. It came very near to me now. Along with it hit my nostrils the scent of his sweat. I could understand that my mama's spirit is now guiding me. Mama came very near to my face and bit my ear lobes as he used to do.

"My dear Abhay Chand, you can tell this monk our love story. I will also accompany you to narrate it. Is that O.K?" Mama's words grew lovelier. The Sufi monk was watching me rubbing my ear lobes as if feeling shy. He could also understand the presence of Sarmad Kashani's spirit around there.

The Sufi monk first paid his obeisance to my mama and then said, "Sadguru, I am deeply honoured by your presence. I am eagerly awaiting to listen to your love story. You may please start first now"

Mama started narrating our love story.

***

The painting depicting the beheaded Sarmad Kashani pronouncing the entire Kalima 'La Ilaha illallah"

Sarmad Kashani- early period of seventeenth century

The captain of the ship-which was on its way from Persia to India- went into the travellers' cabin and announced loudly, "The ship is going to hit the shore shorty. All get ready to alight" Hearing his instructions, the clatter of passengers grew thick. They got busy in picking their belongings from the upper loft and checking their commodities brought from Persia. Some of them were busy walking here and there.

I woke up to the noise of some unruly passengers. A small boy sitting beside me scratched my shoulder out of enthusiasm. "How much longer it would take to reach Hindustan mama?" he asked. Without replying, I kissed him tenderly. A young woman who was sitting in the front at a short distance was watching me without batting her eyes. I looked at myself. My broader hirsute chest was visible outside my upper garment. I adjusted it and saw her having her eyes still fixed upon me.

Getting inquisitive, I looked down casually and was greatly embarrassed at seeing what I saw below my waist cloth…

O! God! I adjusted my waist cloth and lower garment. That woman who was still staring at me chuckled seeing me adjusting my cloths. I rose, hugely embarrassed, and turned my eyes towards other passengers. I was astonished at seeing different types of people on board. They were Persian people travelling on that ship with unending dreams of making a better living for themselves and getting richer after reaching Hindustan along with their families, women and children… There were different types of men on board- Jews, some Parsis, some Greeks, some Arabs, and some Sufis…I was watching the stuff they brought for trade in India, with awe.

There were varieties of woollen bed spreads, woollen dresses, hats, fruits, glasses with intricate carvings, glassware, copperware, items made of iron, and corals...Peregrine falcons used for hunting, mongooses with thick growth of wool, fine-looking fully grown horses, their foals, etc. I was amazed at seeing them all.

I turned again and saw that woman. She was still staring at me heaving a sigh. I diverted my attention and delved into thoughts of my commercial motives. If we were to say something special about the materials produced in Persia, it should be silk that enjoyed popularity that time. The Persian silk industries along the Caspian Sea were manufacturing some of the finest silk materials. Persia exported its quality silk cloths to Russia and other European countries beyond oceans and, in return, it received gold and silver bars in very huge quantity. Even though the domestic production of Persia was relatively low, it was not an exaggerated statement that the favourable geographical location of Persia and its strategically located harbour that functioned as mediating commercial centre connecting Europe and North Asian regions had made Persia an extremely important commercial destination in the world. Persia was accumulating huge wealth through its mediating commerce.

Being located between two big Islamic empires, i.e Hindustan's vast Mughal Empire and renowned Ottoman Islamic Empire of Turkey, our Persia was hugely dependent on these two empires for major part of its commerce. It was a dream of Persian youths those days to go to these Islamic empires, do some business, and earn money to get rich. I was one of those robust young men having such commercial interests in mind.

My name is Sarmad Kashani. As my place of birth was Kashan in Persia, I was known Kashani. The major reason why I had opted for India for doing trade was my spiritual quest for God almighty. I was a Jew by birth. I was proficient in both Jews' language Hebrew and Persian language. It was because of it, I could master the holy book of Jews Torah at very young age. However, Persia where I was brought up fed me the knowledge of Islam. The Islamic education I received from the famous Islamic scholar Mullah Sathra and Said Mir Kasim had made me a perfect Muslim man. But I was deeply inclined more towards Sufism which tried to find out god in one's heart through love without any ostensible strictures than to the extremist Islam which was full of strictures.

The ship reached the shore. I threw my eyes on the items I had brought, examined them once. The chests I brought contained priceless, rare Persian artefacts, rubies, emeralds, and some corals. Along with them were my spiritual books.

"Thatta port has come…the port has come" screamed the small boy. He came to me running. I scooped him up and showered kisses on him. I noticed the boy's father. I was amazed at seeing him having no stuff in his hands like others for doing business. Seeing me amazed, he came forward and offered an explanation to convince me.

"I am ghazal singer. I am good at singing *Kavali* too. I have come to India believing in only my skills in music." '*Some are eccentric like this*' I mumbled myself hearing his words. I alighted from the ship along with my items at Thatta port. The Thatta port situated at the estuary where the river Indus merged with the ocean was once a well-known port for commerce. But it was not like before. The silt brought by the river Indus changed the course of the river which had resulted in Karchi, a nearby harbour, gaining more prominence with huge number of ships anchoring. However, ships, though less in number, did come to Thatta port. In this Thatta port of Sind province, only Hindu merchants were living in large numbers. Due to great efforts of some elder caste Hindu traders who had commercial interests with Arab countries, Thatta port was functional with some ships still using that port for their arrival and departure.

As soon as I alighted from the ship, the coolies surrounded me. As I needed some coolies to carry my luggage, I engaged some of them after a brief bargain. There were many traders hailing from Kashan where I was brought up, doing business extremely well with huge wealth they amassed in Hindustan. I went to their place along with the coolies. I could reach them at last. After a brief sharing of cursory endearing words for each other, I explained them my requirement.

"Friends, all my things are very expensive. So please get me a shop to store and sell those items and a place for me to stay. Within hours, they got me a separate shop and a house just adjacent to it. I got that shop cleaned with the help of coolies I had brought with me and stacked up the items in a manner for easy access while selling them. I got them bring roasted chicken from a nearby restaurant and ate.

As I was very tired due to long journey in ship, I fell asleep. After a deep sleep for long, I could wake up only in the evening. After a complete bath which took away my tiredness, I went out for a stroll. The gentle breeze of the evening was very soothing to my mind. I wasn't sure how long I had enjoyed walking on that street. I thought of returning as I grew tired of walking for a long time. But the ghazal song sung in a sweet voice as if it had reached me by passing through the gentle evening breeze did its part of magic in my heart. I strode fast to the place where the song came from.

It was a big open ground. The dais had been arranged in the middle of it. One of those men on the podium was actually singing the ghazal I was trailing along. Out of curiosity, I went near to him.

"*What a pleasant voice is his!*" I glanced at him near, very intently. I was besotted with his charming face. He was very fair complexioned, sharp noses, tender growth of moustache under his nose, pinkish lips resembling ripe ivy gourd, and extremely softer ear lobes below his big ears. He was still singing, completely unmindful of his surroundings. I was listening to all his modulations closely like a snake that dances to the tunes of snake charmer's trumpet. Brilliant subtleties of ghazal and the elegance of a danseuse manifested in the moves of his hands to arrest all those subtle aspects of ghazal, that magnetic smile on his face as a reflection of his happiness at the thunderous praise of music lovers with their claps when he correctly employs those subtleties of ghazal, his face that gets reddened with that smile and his delicate, fully shaven neck that dances to the tunes of his singing- I was completely dazed, while looking at him, and listening to the verses he was singing.

My masculine cravings awakened now.

Abhay Chand- Thatta port- Early part of Seventeenth century

Mere manu anathu kahan sukku bhave

Where will my heart search for the endless bliss?

Even though the bird living on the ship flies over the ocean

It must come back to the ship. Mustn't it?"

Ignoring the magnificence of Lotus eyed lord Krishna

Would any narrative in search of other gods be right?

Why this madness of digging a well very near to the River Ganga

Just to quench one's thirst?

The main street of Thatta port was celebrating the Sindhi New Year Chethi Chand in a grand manner. It was a festival celebrated to praise the lord Julelal, another incarnation of Varuna, the God of rain. The celebration was conducted with usual grandeur this year too.

My mother is from Rajasthan. She came to Sind province and got married to my father. This song is my mother's most favourite, an ardent follower of Vaishnavite traditions.

As a beloved son who fulfilled her devotional cravings, I was singing that song of devotion and love, composed by saint Surdas for Lord Krishna so passionately on the podium. Other than Hindus who were present there to listen to my song, Muslims, Arabs, Sufis, Jews, and Greeks who all were interested in music had also assembled there. Lord Julelal, celebrated for safeguarding the river Indus had been the only God of Hindus living in Sind province. The Sindhi Muslims living in Thatta port considered Him as their Sufi saint. So, we would sing songs from both Hinduism and Islam.

Sooner I completed singing Saint Surdas's devotional song on Lord Krishna, someone from crowd yelled "Bhaiya, please sing *thama tam mast Kalandar*".

I glanced at the man who shouted from the crowd while sitting on the podium. He was a Muslim. He had come there from a Sufi temple along with his friends to listen to my song. I sang that Islamic song which had been composed in praise of saint Julelal.

"O! Lal meri bat rahiyo balaa julelaan

O! Red clad lord! I am always protected.

O! God of River Indus! O! Our father in Seva town!

Tama tam mast Kalandar"

The crowd now began dancing to the tunes of my song. Hindus, Muslims and others from foreign lands who didn't know our language were among those dancers. The drummer increased his beats so that I would sing the song to match his speed. The festive mood graduated to a different level of frenzy with incomprehensible yells and quickened steps of dance. Today I felt that I had completed singing all the songs satisfactorily. The hand claps and showers of praises took a long time to settle down.

I was watching my mother from the podium. She was immensely happy at seeing me singing with perfection. Completely satisfied with my performance, she disappeared behind the podium to serve food to people who attended the programme. My father was the chairman of the festival committee. He was one among the very prosperous caste Hindu men who ventured out beyond seas and amassed wealth through textile business with Arab countries. The countless number of shops, orchards, bungalows which my father had accumulated for us were not only present in Thatta port but also in many places across Sind province.

This festival would be held for two full days. In order to ensure that the festival went on smoothly, my father was extremely busy with supervising the arrangements made being the chairman of festival committee. It might have been the reason why he couldn't spare time to sit below the podium to listen to me singing. Even now he had gone out on some urgent work. I was left alone on the podium. Many came near the podium and praised me for my performance. One among them, looking taller than me, stood out than the rest. What a masculine appeal he had! Suddenly I started having a tingling sensation akin to that of a mouse running inside me.

His well-built body, sharp eyes, lips that ignited the curiosity like that of plucking the strings of Ektara, dark and thick moustache, plump bearded cheeks that caused fingers restive to pinch- His image got registered in my mind like a painting. He was now coming towards me. I grew edgy seeing him approaching near.

"Wonderful....wonderful..." he poured praises in Persian language with a regal demeanour. Though not well versed in writing Persian, I could speak it fluently. It was true that people who were living, irrespective of races, in Thatta port and its surrounding areas had become proficient in so many languages by way of interacting with the traders arriving at the port for doing business.

"Thanks" – when I reciprocated embarrassingly in Persian, he grasped my hands excitedly. "My name is Sarmad Kashani. I have come from Persia for doing business here." I just bobbed my head. I was literally tongue tied and couldn't even tell him my name. He didn't release his grip from my hands. My tender hands were held under the tight grip of his strong hands. My heart seemed to have been trapped in his hands like a chicken held in the talons of an Eagle. When he shook his hands with mine, I felt his hairs brushing my skin which sent a sudden warmth in me. That mischievous thief did come to know from that warmth what was going through in my heart. The crowd that had arrived in there to listen to my song was still standing near the podium. Some of them went behind the podium for having their meals and serving it to others. Only a few were still waiting near the dais to praise me.

My thief, my wooer, understood the situation. He just said "I will come tomorrow also" and swiftly disappeared. I was still standing unable to come out of my shock. My mother brought me some sweets from the rear of the podium. On the pretext of savouring that sweet I licked my hands where my mischievous man was holding it tightly.

I felt now that the sweet my mother had given me didn't get me satiated.

Sarmad Kashani- Thatta harbour- early part of Seventeenth century.

I didn't know how I walked on and reached the place where I was living. My mind, all the way through, was completely occupied with that boy who sang ghazals. My body became warmer as the passion grew intense. '*Why do I feel such a passionate craving, which I didn't feel even when a woman was gawking at me longingly in the ship, when this Hindu singer sees me intently?*' Reaching my room, I threw my body across the bed. The hairs on my chest that went stiff on seeing the boy had still not returned to its normal state.

I caressed my chest, appeased those stiff strands of hair and comforted myself.

'Who's this boy? I have just lost myself at the very first sight of him? How majestic of a man I am? Where has all that majestic appeal gone in front of him? What a handsome man he is! How attractive he is! What if I could brush his freshly growing moustache with my thick one?'...I couldn't remain on bed after that. I went near to the window, stood along it with my bare chest and tried to cool down my chest exposing it to the chilly wind of sea.

I thought of writing a Rubaiyat verse in Persian. I wrote:

I have been sold in the market of love

Who had bought me?

How much did I cost?

All through that night I remained sleepless. A procession had been scheduled to march from Julelal temple in Thatta harbour to the banks of river Indus. I hoped that I would be able to meet my male sweet heart there.

It took a long time to have a deep sleep.

Abhay Chand- Thatta port- early period of seventeenth century.

I left my home for Julelal temple. When I reached there, I saw a huge crowd had assembled there. Many in the crowd were seen carrying a special plate known as *Bhahrana* brought from their home.

An oil lamp, sugar cubes, a handful of cardamom in heap, fruits, rice mixed with jaggery known as *Akha* were found neatly arranged in the front side of that broad colourful plate. On its other half were found a water jug, coconut, flowers, and an idol of God Julelal. The plate had almost all items neatly arranged that pertained to worshipping of God.

While feeling happy about meeting people who had come to the festival, I had an unusual void of longingness in my heart. I was just wishing the known ones a happy Sindhi New year. Though my body was present there wishing the people around, my mind was searching for my 'mischievous thief'. His face I saw the previous day had been imprinted on my mind. I was unsuccessful in finding him out in that large gathering of people.

The Shobha yatra had also begun. The crowd of devotees started moving slowly, carrying the idol of the god Julelal towards river Indus. The god Julelal shone on a brilliantly decorated palanquin. I bowed my head reverently to pay my respects to Him. The people began dancing Chhej, one of the famous folk dances of Sind province. The *Dandia* dance performed by men standing in circle to the sound of drums and the gleeful clatter of sticks while dancing filled in the air around and rendered the place shine with ecstasy everywhere. Amidst that ecstasy, I grew tired of not being able to find out my secret lover in the crowd. Some Muslim men, Greeks, and Jews joined the dance. Their screams of frenzy in their languages to share their happiness with others had made that procession a marvelous one beyond petty feeling of races and religions.

Unable to find him out, I joined the procession on its one end with an inexplicable burden in my heart. '*He told me that he would come today. Didn't he? Then why didn't he come yet?*' I must have asked this question myself more than thousand times and began to feel that all my enthusiasm had started wearing out. The procession reached the banks of the river Indus. Thousands of men and women had already assembled there. When the procession joined the people already crowded there, they got stampeded out.

I was caught up in that thick crowd where people were standing brushing against other. While standing with a brutal discomfort in the crowd on the river bank I felt someone pressing me with force from behind. I turned back to see who it was. It was my wooer who was pressing me behind. Suddenly I felt an intense gush of excitement flowing like the river Indus in me. I first thanked the God Julelal for uniting me with my beloved man and bowed my head with folded hands.

The crowd grew thicker and crushing me more. Taking advantage of my predicament my beloved man pressed me more from behind and I felt his lips thrusting onto the nape of my neck. The expensive perfume he was wearing on his clothes got me stupefied. He wrote something with his lips on the back of my neck. Every strand of his thick mustache seemed to be drawing picture on that area.

I feigned as if his moustache hurt me and yet leaned more on his side. My head was now on his chest. At the backdrop of stampeding crowd, I could feel that his private part hitting me hard against my buttock. I was about to fall down only to be caught by him. His strong arms caught me from falling down but taking advantage of the situation, they were gently caressing my waist. One of his hands moved above towards my chest. I was left speechless, didn't know what to utter.

"Let it not be here" I murmured in Persian into his ears. "So be it" he said and dragged me away from the crowd. I followed him like a moth that follows light. Soon we reached the place where he was staying. As soon as we entered his room, he grasped my lips with his lips strongly. I cuddled him lovingly, completely oblivious of myself. After some time, we took our clothes off and hugged each other. I rubbed my fully shaven cheeks with his unshaven cheeks desperately. He loved it. He lifted me in his waist and strode to the cot. Sitting on his waist, I was rubbing his big hirsute thighs with my feet. He threw me across the bed and now his whole weight was on my body. His face was scrutinizing the interiors of my arm pits vigorously. The wrestling of two men had just begun on the cot. Like a seasoned wrestler, he enjoyed the way I was wrestling with him and reciprocated my violent, passionate moves. At last it was he won in the game. It took a long time for us to get tired. He then slept like a baby. I once again thanked the god Julelal.

I had never stayed outside my home. For the first time I was going to sleep in the house of my beloved man. I was a little bit worried about my mother who might be concerned about my absence back home.

Sufi Temple. Thatta Port. Sindh Province, Pakistan.

Thatta port, Sindh Province, Pakistan.

Sarmad Kashani- early period of Seventeenth century.

"He and I are same
Like words and their meanings.
We part often and unite often
Like eyes and their sights
Would he part me even a moment?
We will be united everywhere
Like a flower and its fragrance"

Sitting at a place in Thatta port, admiring the vast expanse of the Arabian Sea and thinking of my sweet heart Abhay, I was writing a Rubhaiyat verse. The lenj ship I travelled from Persia had gone back. I didn't go back to Persia in that ship. The only boat in the journey of my life would be none other than Abhay, my male angel. *'I am sitting on this shore waiting for him'*.

It had been ten months now since we, both enjoyed our nearness on the night of *Chet Chand,* the night of the lunar new-year day. We had had cuddled each other countless times after that. We were so used to each other's nudity. We had grown so comfortable with our 'wrestling'. We were proud that we had been the best lovers in the world. The depth of our divine love that had crossed all the language barriers did start on the banks of river Indus and was known to all trees and creepers grown around the Arabian Sea where the river Indus was merging. However, would there be any love affairs that didn't attract criticisms? Some of my friends who saw Abhay Chand visiting my home warned me a couple of times. I preferred not to contradict them as I knew that their warning had the element of truth in it and gave them a silent smile in return.

'Same sex relationship is not something which attracted much of an attention in Sufism. Those who were ridiculing the best poets in Persian language Ameer Khusru and Rumi as 'homosexual poets' are now doing the same to me. Let them speak what they want.' I never got worried about my friends' critical views. On the contrary, I spent my time with Abhay Chand happily.

I could realize that my business was growing dull. All the precious items I had brought along with me had started vanishing one by one from me. But they were nothing in front of my priceless sapphire, my Abhay Chand.

Here he had come for me. Sooner he came to me, he placed his head on my lap. I kissed his forehead gently, gaily. Abhay Chand stroked my hair. We both remained silent for some time, almost unmindful of surrounding enjoying the pleasing caress of each other. At last I broke our silence.

"Abhay Chand, What do you think about spirituality?" I asked him, calmly. Though Abhay Chand was a little surprised at my question which sounded something beyond our love. Yet, he didn't desist himself in replying.

"This Indus River and the Arabian Sea where it merges have seen so many empires and countless religions, Mama. How many religions had set their feet on these plains of Indus River? On one hand, Buddhism nurtured by both China and India. On the other hand, Islam nurtured by Arabs. Beyond that, Judaism cherished by Jews. This side of the river, there are Greeks. Above all, we have Hinduism. Among these religions, which spirituality do you expect me to speak about, Mama?"

I gave out a roaring laughter. '*Abhay Chand, my love, did seem to be no ordinary man. He knew a lot of things.*' I resumed my talk:

"Abhay Chand, I do accept what you ask is right. It is alright. Just tell me what does Hinduism think of spirituality? I don't know much about Hinduism"

Abhay Chand continued:

"Hinduism is not a river that originates at one place and merges at one sea. On the contrary, it was born in places where different languages were spoken, worshipped in different forms of gods, having assumed different patterns of worship and deified as Lord Vishnu, Lord Shiva and Lord Brahma and finally mingling with the universal consciousness, *Paramathma*.". I was watching Abhay in admiration when he was talking with his graceful characteristic expressions.

"We wouldn't be able to find out the origin and end of the river called Hinduism"

Now I grew more interested to know about religions. "Then what..." I was waiting for Abhay Chand to continue.

"*Paramathma* and *Jeevathma* are one and the same. They are the basics of Hinduism. The arguments between these philosophies have been dominating the intellectual space of Hinduism from time immemorial. Many learned men in Hinduism still talk about the philosophical relationships between *Paramathma* and *Jeevathma* in different names namely Advaita, Dwaita and Vashitavaida, Mama"

My interest in knowing more about Hinduism increased. I kept kissing Abhay Chand.

"Abhay Chand, you must do me two favours. First, you should teach me about Hinduism. Secondly, you should give me some books on Hinduism for my better understanding"

Leaning on my chest, Abhay Chand said, "O.K"

I continued. "I will teach you Persian language and Hebrew language of the Jews. You must master these both languages."

"Why should I master those languages, mama?" asked Abhay Chand as he was playing with the hair on my hands.

"I am translating the Torah, the holy book of the Jews from Hebrew to Persian. You should help me in this work. So, you should learn these two languages so as to help me in translating it."

Abhay Chand pulled himself away from me suddenly and stared at me inquisitively.

“Mama, you are a Jew by birth. You do like Torah, the holy book of the Jews. Fine. You have converted to Islam. Due to that you have mastered the holy Quran too. And, now you are ardently following Sufism and visiting Sufi temples. With all these sitting on your back, you are now asking me to teach you Hinduism sitting in front of this Arabian Sea. Why all these? Please explain what do you exactly think of religions of the world?”

Abhay Chand asked me this question like a baby. I pulled him towards me and got his head lain on my lap. With his head on my lap, looking at the sea, I composed a Rubhaiyat poem.

“These religions would lead

the true devotees of god go astray.

The man who suffers from the lesser devotion for god

is nothing but a light of a candle,

to which innocent insects fall prey.

Such light remains same

No matter it is in mosque or Hindu temple”

Abhay Chand asked me as he was lying on my lap. “It just means you don’t like religions. Do you?”

I told, “I don’t despise religions. At the same time I am not very much attached to one particular religion either. You don’t need religion to reach god”

“Where do you think the God is actually dwelling, Mama?” In the sky? On the earth? In temples? Or in mosques?” Abhay Chand asked like an innocent child.

I gazed at Abhay Chand lying on my lap. Those beautiful lips that kindled my desire to bite it…taming my mind which prompted me to travel in different direction, I recited a Rubhaiyat poem once again as a response to his questions.

"The one who dwells only in temples and mosques is not God.

Every creation is His dwelling place.

Even if someone loses his self in the narratives of God

The intelligent ones would always find solace only in the love of god.

Abhay Chand watched me reciting the verse. "What a wonderful thought it is mama! Can I sing this verse in ghazal?" he asked. I nodded yes.

Abhay Chand sang the ghazal as his heart melting out. I wanted to complement his song with the whirling Sufi dance. I rose and danced to his song. The God and his gift to me, my wonderful soul, Abhay Chand, were also dancing in the whirls of my heart. I danced till I grew tired. Abhay Chand came running and hugged me tightly and showered kisses on me. I lifted him and danced again.

The beautiful river Indus merged with the Arabian Sea with its usual roar. Once again, we became one forgetting what we were. We had been so passionately involved that we couldn't realize the presence of an imposing horse standing at a distance with Abhay Chand's father sitting upon it.

Abhay Chand – Thatta port- early period of Seventeenth Century

When I reached home, I saw my home reeling in restiveness. My father was scolding my mother. She remained silent, patiently listening to his jibes with her usual demeanor. I couldn't understand first why he was shouting at my mother. It took some time for me to understand that the affair between I and my mama was the chief cause of that fight. My father avoided talking to me. Without uttering a word, he went upstairs. It was something that had never happened in our house. I was very sad about what had happened.

After some time, my mother came to me. Without speaking anything, she kept staring at my face. '*What is she going to say? Is she also going to hate me like my father? Or would she be able to understand my heart? Would she accept my mama? Why is she staring at me this absorbedly?*' Her penetrating eyes had got me immensely embarrassed. My mother smiled at my embarrassment, seemingly understood what I was going through. She was a devotee of Sadguru Vallabahcharya. She had mastered the philosophy of Pushtimarga Vaishnavite traditions. She was capable of thinking beyond ordinary man-woman relations propounded in that philosophy.

She went into the deity room, brought her Veena, sat down beside me and started plucking its strings. She began singing her most favourite song of Vaishnavite Saint Surdas.

"Shyama Shyamu so hari kelathu ajnabhi

Nandu- Nandan ko Rathe banayee Madhav aab bhaiyee

Saki saga bhaiyee saga saki bhaiyee yosomathi bhavan kaiyi"

--One day Radha played new Holi with Lord Krishna

Krishna became Radha and Radha became Krishna

The women around became men and men around became women

They went to Yasotha's home and danced there

While Yasotha stood astounded at seeing them.

She gave them sweets and was gracefully happy."

That beautiful song she sang proved that she did support what I was. I cried as I was unable to control my overwhelming emotions. My mother didn't cry. She went into the kitchen, came back and extended her hands with sweets. My mother did now appear to me like Mother Yasotha who was happy seeing her son Krishna as woman. I prostrated on her feet and greeted her with my tears. The tears from eyes were flowing down on her ankles.

"Go and meet your father. Get him convinced" she gestured to me with her fingers.

I ran upstairs to meet my father. But my father was not an easy man to get convinced. He was not ready to forgive me like my mother. He kept whining for a long time that all his reputation and status he had earned in society would go in ruins because of me.

"You should never go out anywhere, Abhay Chand. Be at home" he warned me sternly and closed the door with a thud.

Be it present or past, I had never attempted disobeying my father's words. Today too, I remained home having no courage to contradict my father. It was my heart that kept uttering the name of my mama.

Sarmad Kashani- early period of Seventeenth Century.

It had been three month since I last saw Abhay Chand. After I met him at Thatta port, I didn't meet him. I could manage drag one more month thinking that he might be unwell. But even after one month, when he didn't come to meet me, I grew a little worried and became suspicious. I sent a servant to Abhay Chand's house to know about his health.

The servant's reply "okay sir" obviously sounded a tone of mockery. However it didn't get me embarrassed. For me nothing was more important than Abhay Chand. My business, and pejorative remarks of those servants held no much of value before my misery of not being able to meet my sweet heart, Abhay Chand.

Only after receiving the information brought by the servant, I could clearly understand what had exactly happened at Abhay Chand's house. When the servant told me that Abhay Chand wouldn't meet me ever again, I was tremendously confused as to whether should I believe his words or not.

'Abhay was a treasure I received from the god. That treasure would never leave me' I tried comforting my wailing heart, half-heartedly.

I was watching a small boy standing near the opposite shop nagging his mother to buy him a kaleidoscope. How happier he became at once he got the kaleidoscope in hands! When he rolled the pieces of colour bangles inside the tube, he could see different types of beautiful images in it. Though they didn't appear every time he rolled it, kept rolling it in different angles with a renewed excitement to get those beautiful images again without losing hope.

I was unable to forget that beautiful scene. I didn't forget to recite a Rubhaiyat verse even at that time of desolation.

"This world is like a rolling kaleidoscope.

Sometimes hopelessness....sometimes full of hope.

One time it is a spring season...Other times it is an autumn.

Do just forget these fluctuations.

Don't be pained.

Pain is the antidote to pain"

It was true anyway that I was happy simultaneously reciting the verse and watching the boy. Yet all these comforts lasted only for a short time. I was unable to bear the disappointment of not meeting Abhay Chand. My heart ached.

"*Pain is the antidote to pain*" I told myself. I took out a knife from the shop and slashed my hands. The blood gushed like flood. Seeing me, the servant became nervous and ran fast to the adjacent street and brought my friend.

My friend warned me as usual. "My friend, Throw your love away into gutter. Why did you come to India from Persia? Just to bleed and die like this? You have already lost all your wealth and now decided to take away your life as well. Haven't you?"

None of his words could succeed in reducing even a bit of pain I felt in my heart. Leaving aside my shop as it was, I went to my room and locked myself in. I threw myself on bed. "*I must do something to get back my dearest Abhay*" my mind kept repeating this again and again. I regained my composure and began thinking deeply.

"No matter how big my attempts are, I wouldn't be able to convince Abhay's father whose sole motive in life is nothing other than being conscious of his social status. The rules of religion in this society would never allow us live together peacefully. Both spirituality and Abhay Chand are very important to me" I kept pondering…pondering till I developed a mental fatigue. It was then I took that sudden decision.

I took all my clothes off. I let loose my lock of hair which I hadn't trimmed for days. I quietly stroked my thick beard which I hadn't shaven since long.

I opened the door and walked onto the street, stark naked. Stray dogs on the street found me intriguing and barked at my nudity. Some boys threw stones at me. Only some of them came near, touched my phallus and revered it. It was Sindh province where nudity was also worshiped in the form of god.

But nothing affected me. I ran out on the street shouting Abhay's name. "Abhay Chand…Abhay Chand". Even in that critical juncture, I didn't fail to recite a rubhaiyat poem.

"That extremely handsome man has his rule over me.

He, an extraordinary thief, has rendered me nude"

I sang the poem aloud and ran out on the street nude. Having learnt about me, some of my friends came running after me.

"Sarmad, what happened to you? Why do you roam mad?" they threw a rug over me and tried to cover my nudity. I prevented them from doing it and sang more Rubhaiyat poems.

"There is nothing wrong in this mad man.

All the mistakes are yours.

Love has not yet made you all mad"

They came behind me again and covered my body with the rug. I slid off that rug again, threw it away on the floor and ran out naked on the street.

Unable to control me, my friends stood still.

Abhay Chand- Thatta port- early period of Seventeenth Century

'How many days will I be confined like this in this room? Why does the big garden lying behind my house look barren now? Why does the 'lolo' confection, which my mother used to make exclusively for me as I loved it more, taste bitter now? Why does the Ektara, which gave my mother peace of mind when I played it, carry such a sullen face and cry now?'

My heart is in inexplicable pains like a camel which looks out for water on these vast deserts of Sindh province. I didn't know answers to any of my questions. I was simply lying on bed almost unconscious. That time, I heard my father arguing loudly with someone outside my house. I peeked through the window and saw my mama standing nude there.

I sprinted to the entrance. My mother had already reached there. She remained undisturbed by the nudity of mama. Being ardent follower of Hinduism, my mother was very much familiar with the nakedness of Hindu sadhus. Mama looked into my father's eyes and spoke:

"Sir, what you saw me along with your son that day is completely different from that of one you see today. This nakedness is the beginning of getting into Sanyasa. I am just a spiritual seeker who tries to figure out the intimacy with god through the means of love and meditation unlike others who seek God through religions."

"Even the so-called messengers of god propounded by religions had faced the phenomenon called lust, a typical human trait at least at one point of time in their life and fought it and transcended it. As a spiritual seeker, I also share similar experience. Abhay Chand is the companion of my passion. He is just a follower of my spiritual quest."

"You are not aware of my spiritual power. Had I thought, I could have abducted your son with my spiritual power. But I don't prefer doing that. I am standing nude as a mendicant in front of you just to earn your trust on me. This is the stage of Sanyasa where I have abdicated all my wealth and comfort." Mama spoke in his firm silvery voice.

My father didn't speak anything. I looked at him. His eyes were burning red with anger. Sarmad mama continued:

"Please have some patience to listen to what I am saying. Your son Abhay Chand was not born to become a merchant like you. He is also a spiritual seeker. We stand for each other just to transcend lust, an obvious obstacle on the path to attain spirituality. Lust is not our ultimate goal. Our ultimate goal is love. Our goal is to reach god. I will save your son. You can trust me"

Without responding to mama, my father turned and looked at me. I was almost torn between my love and my father. Nevertheless, I was prepared to go with mama.

My father could understand that his son Abhay Chand had gone out of his hand and didn't like to stand an obstacle anymore between us. Now he spoke:

"It had just happened as it was destined to. I have lost my son anyway. It is an intolerable pain in my life. Being a rich man, I have a status to count on. I want you both to get out of my sight by going to some unknown place. Scandalous talk of people still does matter to me"

My mother cried inconsolably. My parting from her was an unbearable agony for her. Yet, she seemed to be happy and at peace that her beloved son had got something in his life which he liked most. She wept for a while and bid me adieu.

I parted my mother. I followed my mama like Sita who went to forest following the footsteps of Lord Ram.

Tomb of Sarmad Guru in front of Jumma Masjid, Delhi. (Exterior)

Tomb of Sarmad Guru in front of Jumma Masjid, Delhi. (Interior)

Abhay Chand- later part of seventeenth century

In the middle of forest where no humans lived, I was busy collecting dried twigs for cooking lunch. Mama was sitting in a nearby cave and meditating.

There used to be a lot of servants in my home in Thatta port to do such works. But here I had to do all those works myself and the satisfaction I derived from it was something indescribable in words. I came back to our hut with the bundle of twigs I collected. Mama, still sitting in the cave, hadn't competed his prayer. I was watching my dear Mama from a distance.

'Which God is he praying to in his solitary meditation? Is it Yahweh alias Jehovah, the chief god of Judaism in which he was born? Or is it Islam's Allah? Or is it Ram of Hinduism?' My thoughts paced to the past.

After leaving my home, we first went to Lahore. It was not easy to get an accommodation in Lahore for me and my mama who roamed nude. The society which was so derisive in its way of approaching nudity while someone walking on streets did not make any such overt complaints while entering temples nude. So we stayed in temples. My mama, whose quest for spirituality grew extremely intense, was patient enough to teach me Persian and Hebrew, the language of the Jews. As a sincere disciple obedient to his master, I learnt those two languages.

I helped my mama in translating the spiritual treasure of Jews- Five texts of their holy book Torah- Genesis, Exodus, Leviticus, Numbers, and Deuteronomy into Persian language. The way Lord Ram's struggles in the forest got registered in my mind, the struggles of the god's children Moses an Elia mentioned in Torah also got registered in my mind. I learnt the holy Quran and the tenets of Islam from mama. I used to listen to him very eagerly when he narrated the five pillars of Islam- Kalima, Prayer, Fasting, Sahad, and Hajji. Mama, in turn, would ask me lots of questions on Hinduism. Among other religions he liked Hinduism most for its accommodative trait in revering nudity.

Mama loved the philosophy of *Advaita* which says *Paramathma* and *Jeevathma* are one and the same and Jeevathma can graduate to Paramathma if it is willing. This philosophical stand which almost resonated the Sufi philosophy that God is one, did prompt mama to delve into deeper inquiry on Hinduism. *Nirkuna Brahmam*, a stage in which God takes no form, and ways of worshiping *Nirkuna Brahmam* in different definite forms, a stage of *Sakuna Brahmam* explained in Hinduism got my mama intrigued profoundly and he had discussed these matters with me very frequently.

But I never discussed the bigger evils, caste and discriminations prevailing in Hinduism with him. My Sarmad Mama who had profound understanding in Sufism and Islam asked me multi-layered questions on Hinduism and at one point it was evident that he had become a Hindu himself. One day he recited a Rubhaiyat verse in lighter vein about this change in his mind.

"O! Sarmad,

You, the one who turned atheist souls

To Allah's Islam.

Now, what defects have you found in Allah

and his messenger

That you have become

a disciple of Ram and Laxman?"

I could understand from his poem the miserable state of a poor man who was persistently searching for god in every religion. Sometimes Mama's spiritual quest would be abnormal. I would caress his chest to assuage the heat of his quest. My guru, my mama would then become a child in my hands. I would lie on his nude lap like a baby. His passions would then be awake. I would touch my eyes with his magnificent erect phallus. The soul which had been busy searching for the spiritual knowledge would search for something in my body fervidly during such nights.

He would utter some '*mantra*' into my ears, then on my neck, then on my arm pits, then on my nipples, then on my naval and search for some fathomless phenomenon in me. One day in such a frenzy of quest on body, mama recited a brilliant Rubhaiyat verse.

"You are my companion in my journey on the road

You are my guide to the path I am searching for.

Whoever I talk, you will remain its reply.

If the sun calls upon the moon to the sky

It is you who comes first and shines there.

In my solitary nights, you are my only solace.

If I laugh, you will be the smile on my lips

If I cry, you are the tears on my face.

If I write, you become the sentence

If I sing, you stand there as song.

At any time, if I search for another lover

It is you who enters in him too."

We never confused mama's *Sanyasa* with our sexual relationship. Moses, the God's messenger in Judaism was leading a happy life with his wife. Prophet Mohammed, the god's messenger in Islam, led his life with his wives. My mama, who had literally renounced all the worldly pleasures actually considered our relationship a divine one.

Some other day, one of his devotees asked him, "Who's your god?" "Here is my god", he replied pointing to me. He was such a soul who took pride in our relationship and singing Rubhaiyat songs for me.

Only the fundamentalist Muslims who lived by the tenets of the Shariyat laws did hate my mama's nudity. The Muslims following Sufi Islam and were liberal in thoughts in fact found Sarmad Kashani mama's spiritual knowledge enticing.

Sarmad Kashani mama was always surrounded by a large number of Muslims who didn't consider nudity an issue and the Hindus who considered nudity as a manifestation of divinity. This crowd remained captivated by his talk, mama's exquisite appeal and knowledge. But mama's quest remained incomplete as he was still searching for the god, the magnificent.

Being near to him, I was watching his growing anxiety towards finding god. With my hugs, I kept his spiritual anxiety cool down. After ten years of living such life, mama undertook a journey to Deccan region, to Hyderabad. I followed him. The number of customers visiting a diamond merchant who sells only diamonds would always be lesser when compared to the number of customers visiting a merchant who sells other gem stones including diamonds, corals, sapphires, and rubies. Mama's spiritual knowledge was akin to such gem stone sellers.

Since all the gem stones such as the Torah- a diamond, Islam- a lapis Lazuli, Buddhism-an emerald, Hindusim- a garnet, Christianity-a coral, were lying with one noble man called Sarmad Kashani, a very large number of devotees was thronging to see him. The presence of a nude saint called Sarmad Kashani became a much talked about topic everywhere. Those who were in genuine quest for god did find Kashani mama an irrefutable source of spiritual knowledge.

He was accorded the highest regard by people usually given to a complete Sufi saint, Kalandar. Saint Kalandar was not confined to a particular religion and didn't have anyone as his Guru. The journey of Saint Kalandar didn't have any fetters designed by religions. On the contrary, the one who attained the state of being a Kalandar would have only god, devotee, and the exquisite love between them. It was this state of Kalandar, mama had been striving for every day.

In all spiritual pursuits in search of god, god's messengers could attain higher enlightenment only after being virtually pushed into solitude. Some of them who attained such a stage had declared themselves gods too. My mama who had been in search of god every day seemed to be undergoing similar trials.

Like the great souls who attained enlightenment in solitude such as Buddha who got enlightened under Bodhi tree, Jesus Christ whose patience was tried in hot desert for forty days, Moses who received the ten commandments of God being in solitude on Sinai hills, Prophet Mohammed who received profound knowledge of God in Hira caves, I and my mendicant mama Kashani had come to this forest area from the Deccan region to attain enlightenment in solitude.

Most of the times, mama meditated in solitude. I cooked only for myself. Though I preferred not to disturb the spiritual efforts of mama, I couldn't help feeling sad seeing him undergoing enormous physical pain in his spiritual pursuits. After a long time of solitary meditation, mama came out of the cave. I offered him some water as he was visibly tired.

"Did you see God in your meditation?" I asked him.

"No" he replied.

"Islam, Hinduism, Buddhism and Torah- through your meditation, were you able to realise any one of the Gods mentioned in these religions as real?"

“No” mama replied.

“Even after having mastered the teachings of Abraham, Moses, Jesus Christ, Prophet Mohammed, Lord Ram, Laxman, and Buddha, you didn’t find anyone in your meditation? Did you?”

“Yes, I didn’t find” mama replied.

I was caught surprised at his replies. “Are you telling there is god? Or simply negating it?”

Mama didn’t reply to this question too.

I was left tremendously confused. Before my confusion got dried up, I added one more question. “Mama, are you an atheist who denies the existence of god?”

Mama now replied calmly.

“There are two types of atheists in the world. First type of atheist is the one who flatly denies the existence of god universally accepted by the world. Another type of atheist is the one who had the audacity to declare he is god himself. By declaring himself as god, he indirectly denies the existence of gods accepted in this world, and thus he becomes an atheist too.”

I was stunned at his reply. I grew excited thinking whether mama had become an atheist of second type who thinks himself as God.

“Mama, are you a god?” when I asked this question excitedly, he intervened and told:

“Love is god. The heart in which god dwells is His abode. God is within me. If you search for Him, he will be within you too”

"The flame from a candle would remain same in emitting its light no matter it is in temple or mosque. The light of lamp called God would always be bright everywhere. When the light is in your heart, its brightness will be immensely profound. Even now I am not very comfortable in declaring me as god. I am a confused man, who still perceives god embodied in theism from an atheistic point of view."

Mama got up and walked on. I paced behind him.

"We are going to Delhi tomorrow" Mama told and kissed me. I set off to look after the arrangements for the journey.

Harem of Prince Dara Shiko

Dara Shiko, debating Upanishads with Hindu saints.

The prince Dara Shiko- Palace of Emperor Shahjahan- Delhi

The one which we can't see,

The one that gives power to eyes to see things

Is what we must know as God.

Anything preached as God

Can never be God. (Keno Upanishad)

Eyes can't reach Him.

But it is He who reaches everyone's eyes

He possesses sharp and flawless enlightenment.

(Al Quran 6:103)

In that big silent hall of the palace, I was discussing, comparing the Upanishads of Hinduism with the teachings of the holy Quran. The hall was filled with Hindu saints who I had brought from Varanasi to translate the texts from Sanskrit to Persian, the Sufi saints who loved singular philosophy of God and liberal spirituality and Islamic scholars praising the Shariyat laws. I talked, composed myself:

"Dear courtiers, learned men, I have translated this Hindu spiritual text called Yoga Nishta from Sanskrit into Persian with the help of these Hindu scholars. When I proposed to translate this book, two great men in solemn countenance appeared in my dream". The hall fell into pin drop silence when I uttered these words. The crowd assembled to discuss spiritual matters in that hall sharpened its ears and paid close attention what I was to say. I resumed my talk.

"The first one standing above was Rishi Vashishta and the one standing below was Lord Ram". As they heard these names pronounced, the Hindu Sadhus sitting in the assembly gently patted their cheeks with a mild chant '*Ram…Ram*'. The Sufis whose quest for god was through the means of spirituality, evinced interest in what I was going to say. Only those Islamic scholars defending the Shariyat laws were sitting tight faced listening to my words. Their harsh expression showed that they didn't like me talk those words being the prince of Mughal Empire, who was brought up as a Muslim. I just ignored it and resumed my talk.

"Rishi Vashishta who came in my dream held my back lovingly and told Lord Ram, "Ram, he is our brother who is genuinely interested in knowing the magnificent truth about God. Hug him tightly". Lord Ram hugged me with immense love and affection. Later, rishi Vashishta offered lord Ram some sweets. Lord Ram received it with high regards and I picked some of it from his hands. My dream ended therewith"

Some in the assembly howled enthusiastically. Some wrinkled their face. I continued my talk. "Dear learned men, it was only after that dream I translated this book, Yoga Vashishta into Persian with the help of some of my servants who are proficient in the language. Our Hindu Sadhus helped me by supervising the quality of the translation. I thank them all. When I said that I had mentioned about the dream in the preface I had written for Darjuma and Yoga Vashishta, one Kalima intervened and said, "Most pampered son of the emperor Shahjahan, our prince Dara Shiko, do you understand that you are journeying against the basic tenets of Islam which say Allah is the only god?" his voice brimmed with anger.

A Hindu Sadhu sitting on the opposite side asked me politely, "Prince, What is your purpose of translating Hindu scriptures into Persian? Do you want to show this world that Hindu religion is better than Islam?"

I got slightly angry. I stared at the Ulema who spoke arrogantly and the Hindu Sadhu who spoke bigheadedly and replied. "First of all you must understand this translation of spiritual texts is beyond religions. My books are not written for those petty religious fundamentalists who seek omniscient god in the pages of books. My translations are written for real spiritual seekers who search for god almighty beyond religions. The religious fundamentalists who think their beliefs can only prevail over everything would always contradict me. On the other hand, those real spiritual seekers who think God is ever present in every religion in any form would always admire me. The crowd got slightly excited, stirred hearing this. Ignoring it, I continued my talk.

"I am like my grand-father Emperor Akbar. Emperor Akbar had an in-depth understanding of similarities and dissimilarities among religions. He revolutionised religions by founding 'Tin Ilahi', a combined set of religious rules drawn from various religions. Those religious fundamentalists who opposed him are now opposing me as well." The crowd grew more agitated.

One of the Ulemas yelled at him angrily. "Prince of Mughal Empire! You have already translated fifty Hindu Upanishads into Persian language. You have given it a title "Shir e Akbar" meaning 'profound secret'. Could you please tell this court where is that profound secret you have mentioned to describe Hindu Upanishads found in the holy Quran?" I maintained my composure even when he blurted that question in anger.

"As far as I am concerned, it is my humble opinion that '*Kitab al Makhn*' mentioned in the holy Quran is nothing but the secret lessons of Upanishads mentioned in Hindu religion taught by a Guru to his disciple."

The Ulemas grew further agitated. Some of them even threatened that they were going declare Dara Shiko, the Prince, the son of Emperor Shahjahan a kafir, an infidel in public.

I didn't lose my patience yet. "Dear Ulemas, the learned men who follow the Shariyat laws, please do have patience to listen to what I want to say. Before translating these books, I had already narrated the life histories of forty Islamic Sufi saints in one of my books called '*Sabinat ul Avliya*'. After that, I have written four Islamic Sufi books like '*Sabinat ul Avliya*'. Without devotion to Allah, how would I be able to write them all? Don't forget one thing. Religions are not important to me. Only god is important to me."

The Ulemas did not agree with my arguments. "Those, who dance and sing in the name of *Diggir* at the time of prayer in mosques where one has to pray silently, are not the children of Allah. The books written about them are not books anyway" - an Ulema quoted a sentence from the Quran.

"Utter the name of god

On every morning and evening

With politeness and fear.

Think about god without making noise" (Al Quran 1-205)

"As a prince of this country you must accept those, who sing and dance in the mosques forgetting this sentence from the Quran, cannot be the children of Allah. You must not forget that you are inviting the wrath of learned Mullahs who teach righteousness with your inclination to hold onto other religions on an equal pedestal with Islam."

Hardly had I heard those words, my anger crossed its threshold. I mocked at those Mullahs.

"Mullahs are not present in the heaven

Their squirms and noisy complaints wouldn't be there

Let this world be freed from the Mullahs' fundamentalism

Let no one care about their Fatwa

No intelligent man would be found in where Mullahs live."

All of them screamed in unison and walked out of the hall. I grew extremely angry. Had it been a battle field my sword could have done its part by now. Since it was a hall where spiritual matters were discussed, I had to be patient. Not knowing how to control my raging heart, I became restive.

That time, a guard came in and announced, "Revered Prince, Sarmat Kashani has arrived in. He is waiting for you outside". I was greatly happy to receive that news. I took that opportunity in my favour to dilute the hot, hostile ambience in the hall. "Dear learned men, we may meet tomorrow. Our meeting is over today". The assembly disbursed and left the hall.

When Sarmad Kashani entered the hall, I paid my obeisance and held his nakedness in high regard.

"My humble greeting Guru. I had two Sufi saints as my teachers till yesterday. One is Mian Mir from Lahore, my senior teacher and the other is Mullah Shat Badakshi, the disciple of my senior Guru. Now along with them, I have got Saint Sarmad Kashani as my third teacher. I am blessed to have you as my guru" My head bowed in utmost reverence and greeted.

Kashani blessed me. I watched the handsome youth standing beside him. The feminine grace of that boy looked embarrassed at my sharp scrutinising eyes. I greeted that disciple gifted with feminine refinements with a warm smile, "You are welcome, Abhay Chand".

Sarmad guru looked at me fixedly. "O! The prince of this vast Mughal Empire. Your face says you are deeply worried about something. May I know why?", he asked. I explained him in detail the hot debate I had a while ago with Ulemas. Sarmad guru laughed his heart out. His long pendulous phallus was swinging from side to side when he laughed.

I turned to Abhay Chand. He, with his feminine elegance, was very focussed only in attending to his master. '*What a devotion towards his teacher*! Sarmad guru now spoke.

"My dear prince Dara Shiko, it is extremely difficult to prove the fact that neither you nor I ever denied Allah, the god almighty, to these ignorant blokes whose knowledge of the Holy Quran is no way beyond just treating it a book. They won't understand the principles of Sufism that any clarity of spiritual matters in Islam about Allah holds significance only if it is taught by a Sufi saint to his disciples. And, they won't accept our belief being Sufis that Prophet Muhammad is the first Sufi saint. In this backdrop, they...." Sarmad Guru paused. I watched him absorbedly as to know what he was about to say next.

"In this back drop, any of your insinuation spoken out one step ahead indicating that your research findings on Upanishads- they are the secret teachings of Hindu Saints to their disciples -would definitely infuriate the Ulemas who have already been terribly angry with you, prince"

I acceded to what Sarmad Guru told. I wanted to pay more attention to his words. Sarmad Guru resumed.

"Just like Hindu religion which strives to reach god through meditation, we find happiness in looking for god in one's heart in Sufi Islam. Just like Hindu religion which tries to reach out to god through songs and dances, we Sufis pray to god through Sufi dances. As these two religions share some commonalities, we are more inclined to appreciate Hindu religion. On the other hand, those who look for strictures in the Quran to define ordinary essentials of human life-food one eats, dress one wears, words one speaks, the way eyes see others, the way ears listen, and body that passionately loves others-would find us Kafirs, infidels and it wouldn't be surprising anyway. However, my dear prince…" Sarmad Guru spoke in a cautionary tone.

"I am just a mendicant owning nothing. Even if people abuse me as Kafir, it will leave no effect on me. But you are the prince of this country, would be crowned tomorrow as king. You are not the only son to the Emperor Shahjahan. You, the eldest among your brothers, are a liberal Sufi follower whereas you your younger brother Aurangazeb is a hard core Islamic religious man who does everything to keep the Shariyat laws relevant. Another brother follows a different sect of Islam, Shia Muslims. You must understand it is your penchant for bringing out Hindu scriptures in translation is going to be the main cause of rift with your two brothers who might soon pose imminent danger to you and your crown"

I agreed with his words. "Master, it is true what you say. There is an impending danger from my two brothers. But, master, I am a soldier…it is his strong faith in my valour, my father Shahjahan has given me the complete charge of a very big army with a big cavalry and innumerable war elephants. I have never betrayed his faith till now. So I am not intimidated by these life threats anyway. But my question is only one" I paused. Sarmad guru gestured to me to continue.

"Can't anyone who thinks beyond religions be a king of this land, master?"

Sarmad guru grinned at my question.

"We need supports for creepers to grow high. Kings are needed for religions to flourish. Dear prince, you are not an ignorant man who doesn't know history"

"In this world, it is religions and religious extremists that had been behind many wars and the kings who fought it"

"When there is no justifiable reason to topple a government, it is religion that becomes an only easy tool for humans to topple a good government. This is the truth taught by yester year history. This is the truth being taught by present history. Tomorrow's history will also teach the same, prince. Do give a thought on what I say. Your grandfather Emperor Akbar could introduce a new religious doctrines called 'Tin Ilahi' into Hindustan only after expanding his empire. Had he spoken of those newly found religious doctrines immediately after his ascension to thrown, this Mughal Empire could have got reduced to nothing by now. So dear prince, without religions there couldn't be kings. At the same time, those who think beyond religions can certainly be kings. Now what are you, a would-be-king, supposed to do? Keep religions at bay. Always be cautious about extremists"

I could fully appreciate the logical concerns in his words. I was very lucky to have him as my master. Our talk shifted to other topics. I learnt from him many things about Jews' Torah book. I was surprised to see Sarmad Guru was more erudite in his understanding on differences of religions than me. How much longer could we talk only about spiritual matters? We had tea together. Only that time, Abhay Chand opened his mouth to speak.

"Prince, other than spiritual matters, your interest in painting is something phenomenal. Can I see your paintings, prince?"

I felt like falling in love with Abhay chand seeing him speak shyly.

"Sure" I told him, and led them to the room where my paintings were kept.

Abhay Chand was watching all my paintings and stood dumbfounded at seeing two paintings- one in which I was sharing bed with women, flirting with them and another which depicted a hunting scene.

It looked funny seeing him watch the painting of my flirts with women without batting his eyes. He regained his senses only after I patted his shoulder.

"While you love spirituality, it is evident from your paintings that you love women too. Do you like women more?" Abhay Chand asked me.

I smiled at him and replied, "I love hunting women. Spirituality is inherent to lust, Abhay Chand."

"Please explain it in detail" Abhay Chand's questions ignited my passionate longings more.

"A powerful weapon is the most important requirement of hunters for a good hunt. Next most important requirement is his skill in throwing that powerful weapon at targets without missing it. The last important requirement is to savour the remains of animals he hunted." Abhay Chand grew red, probably with the fire of lust in him, listening to my double meaning talk.

Now I started teasing Sarmad guru. "Master, can you please tell me about your experience in *hunting*?? Sarmad threw a grin at me and told glancing at Abhay Chand.

"My *hunt*...here is standing in front of you. Its ears are my venison. Its cheeks are my goat meat. Its neck is my beef. Prince, I have been savouring different types of dishes everyday" I laughed out aloud at his witty reply.

"Abhay Chand, what about your experience?" I asked Abhay Chand.

"O! My goodness!" Abhay Chand covered his face with his palms. Sarmad master continued.

"Abhay Chand is a vegetarian. One day I may look him as a banana tree, other day guava fruits and grapes and some vegetables, I guess."

The hunting scene painted by Dara Shiko

"Our prince describing women with the hunted animals is a matter of peculiar taste. It is a matter of discomfiture too"

With the whiff of liquor, that day ended.

Everyone laughed at his funny reply. Abhay Chand too accompanied us in our joyful moments and told amidst laughter.

Aurangazeb's court, with the beheaded head of Dara Shiko.

Sarmad Kashani- Delhi- later period of seventeenth century

In early morning, people living on the street around Jumma Masjid were running helter shelter, howling helplessly. I got up to that huge uproar from my sleep.

"The prince Dara Shiko has been arrested. Good heavens! Our prince is in the hands of a tyrant. O! god! Some women yelled aloud, crying desolately. The dust kicked off from street as the cavalry men of Aurangazeb entered with their tough horses.

"Calm down...calm down..." the soldiers shouted. But no one seemed to obey their orders. The situation looked very volatile. I understood everything. *'The history of Hindustan that went on uneventful till now is going to be written differently. Hindustan has gone into the hands of a man who knows nothing about living in unity.'* I leaned against the wall and sat down. I couldn't happily drink the tea Abhay Chand made for me with love. The prince Dara Shiko fully occupied my mind. After my meeting with the prince Dara shiko, I had witnessed many changes in Delhi. There were innumerable feuds and conflicts between the pure spiritualist Dara Shiko and his extremist brothers for the throne.

Since I came to Delhi, I and Dara Shiko had become bosom friends commonly connected by our spiritual quest. During those days when I roamed around declaring that god is one, He is Allah, He is Lord Ram, He is Jesus Christ, it was the prince Dara Shiko who stood behind me and extended his support. *'Today, that prince Dara Shiko, has been arrested, thrown into the hands of a religious fanatic.'* It was soothing to see the people of Delhi stand on our side.

Internecine conflicts among emperor Shajahan's sons became evident in public from the day the king announced that he had been keeping unwell. King's support lay behind his elder son Dara Shiko. Only with this staunch support, Daro Shiko could defeat his first younger brother Shah Sujha with the help of his son Humayun Shiko in a war at Bhagadurpur.

But it was terrible pity that Dara Shiko's courage didn't help him to fight Aurangazeb, the third son of the emperor. Dara Shiko had to run away to Lahore after being defeated by Aurangazeb in the second fierce battle at Samugar. He then roamed like a nomad from Lahore to Thatta port in Sindh, and then to Gujarat and at last met the governor of Gujarat Navas Khan. He recruited his army with the help of the governor and went to fight with his brother Aurangazeb at Ajmer. This time too, Aurangazeb routed Dara Shiko in the battle.

Heart-broken, Dara Shiko ran away again to Sindh. But this time his destiny took him to Malik Jwan. Once upon a time, when this Afghan Malik Jwan was defeated by Dara Shiko's father Shahjahan and rendered him defenceless, it was the prince Dara Shiko who had saved his head. But the destiny had some other plan. Malik Jwan's fake friendship proved very dear as he betrayed Dara Shiko and got him arrested by Auragazeb's soldiers. Dara Shiko, a pearl of spiritual pursuits, was brought to Delhi as prisoner.

"Down with Malik Jwan…Down with Malik Jwan, the traitor who betrayed our prince Dara Shiko" louder yells of people filled in the streets of Delhi. The huge uproar was accompanied by the uneven sounds of horse hooves as the cavalry of Aurangazeb was trying to control the mob frenzy.

I felt it was not advisable to venture out nude at this critical time. I sent out Abhay Chand to collect the information about the events unfolded on the streets of Delhi.

Abhay Chand- Delhi- later part of seventeenth century

I was running along with other people in the crowd to reach the place where Dara Shiko was kept confined. A big crowd had already assembled there as I reached the spot. In the middle of the crowd, four quasi judges in dark clad and many Ulemas with their ever-ready skulls to bob at every word of Aurangazeb, were sitting. The Princess Rosanna was also sitting majestically amidst them. She had also turned to be an arch enemy of her own brother Dara Shiko. What a pity!

The prince Dara Shiko, who was brought up with milk and honey anointments and on spongy mattresses in the palace was now treated like an ordinary slave prisoner after being stripped off his upper clothes and was standing half nude.

First quasi asked him, "Dara Shiko, take the ring off from your fingers and hand it over to me". The prince obeyed his words. The quasi rolled that ring, fidgeting it a while in his fingers and retorted, "On one side of this ring, it is written Allah. On the other side, it is written Lord. Do you mean to say Hindu god is equal to Islamic god Allah?"

Dara Shiko raised his head and said, "Honourable men, the one who created this world has many names. We call Him god. We call Him Allah. We call Him Lord Ram. We call Him Jehovah. We call Him Ahura or Majda. We call Him in different names."

"You mean that Allah worshipped by Muslims is equal to the gods Hindus worship. Don't you?" the quasi repeated his question.

"Yes. I believe that Allah, the god almighty is known in different names in the world. I believe that the god who has created this world is only one. I believe that he is being worshipped in different names in different places" This reply from Dara Shiko created a stir among Ulemas assembled there.

Next quasi asked him, "Do you want to deny the accusation that the Sanskrit scholars you brought from Varanasi to translate Hindu scriptures into Persian had done their job on your orders?"

Dara Shiko was composed, and offered the judge a polite reply, "No…I don't. I was the one instrumental in translating those Upanishads"

The judge became angry. "So, you dare compare the Hindu holy scriptures with the holy Quran? Am I right?" Dara Shiko intervened the judge and told, "I have just compared them only on the basis of their contents. I would like to register my views here that those two books are entirely different from each other in their appeal. The holy words in every religion contain priceless life philosophies in them. This is what I am trying to say here, hon'ble jury"

He continued, "Hon'ble Jury, It is not something you are unaware of. The holy Quran says, Allah the merciful, had sent his one hundred twenty-four thousand messengers to this world. The holy messages of Allah uttered by these messengers do not belong only to Islam. I believe that they belong to all religions. When these messages are transferred to other languages, I believe, it loses its originality and take the shape one's whims due to confusions in languages and religions. In order to avoid such misunderstandings, a comparative study among religions assumes importance. This has only necessitated those translations, hon'ble judge". Despite being eloquent in its contents, this reply failed to convince the quasi judge.

The quasi judge continued asking questions in an attempt to know the deep spiritual friendship that Dara Shiko shared with Sikh gurus.

"Are you still believing that the root of Sikh people's faith in god actually got its origin in Islam and Hindu religions?" the judge asked Dara Shiko.

"I do believe so, hon'ble judge. Sikhs respect both Islam and Hindu religions"

The judge didn't stop with that, and told further. "Guru Nanak, a Sikh guru, says that the quasi judges who are to deliver justice hold a rose in one hand and keep the name of god on their lips, do abuse justice if they are not given bribe in their other hand. And, if someone opposes their wrong justice, they run to the Holy Quran and scrutinize every page of it to pick some words that would sanction taking revenge against the person opposing their judgement. Are all these accusations by Guru Nanak true?"

Dara Shiko replied calmly. "There may be some elements of truth in it. Sometimes the critical views of some religious scholars criticising other religions and their so-called spiritual growth do not go hand in hand, hon'ble judge."

Now the judge fumed, "Most of the times you are ridiculing Mullahs and quasi judges of your religion. Not once. Many times. Is that true?"

Dara Shiko was silent for a while. It appeared that he needed some space for regaining his composure. He resumed his talk, more poised now. "Hon'ble judges, which sentence in the Holy Quran which we revere most says the Mullahs and quasi judges should be placed in high regards? Their names are mentioned nowhere. You are well aware that the messenger of god and Islam do not require such intermediaries. Hon'ble judge, I have never criticised anyone. I have just been critical about those men who boast of themselves as representatives of god. Could you ever show a place in the holy Quran where Mullahs, Moulvis, Imams are referred to as Allah's representatives?"

This reply from Dara Shiko stirred the hornet nest as some in the court shouted in high pitch. There followed a pandemonium in the court as other Mullahs joined the people yelling. They, the haters of Dara Shiko, hurled hate-filled invective at Dara Shiko.

"Would you all please shut your mouth?" the princess Rosanara's commanding voice subdued the crowd. The crowd stood quiet now.

"Why this unnecessary argument with this fool? He is an infidel and give him punishment he deserves. The punishment given to him should be a lesson for others who dare to insult Islam"

The dreaded crowd remained silent, awaiting the events scheduled to be unfolded in a while. Only the quasi judges went to the adjacent room to meet Aurangazeb. They returned after a long time carrying the order of Aurangazeb, and passed their judgement- Dara Shiko should be executed.

I wept at the pronouncement of judgement. It was very distressing to see a good man being punished for his ill destined life. I could no longer stay there more and trudged fast to reach the street near Jumma Masjid where Sarmad Kashani mama was staying. I saw a crowd assembled there, visibly in mourning.

Sarmad Kashani- Delhi- Later part of Seventeenth Century.

Today there were a lot of devotees arrived in my place to discuss the injustice meted out to Dara Shiko. Irrespective of their faiths, the crowd was a motley representation from Hindus, Muslims, and Sikhs. I could see some Ulemas were also there in the group. A Hindu Sadhu from the crowd spoke first. "Sarmad guru, you are a very close friend of the prince Dara Shiko. He had been our prince blessed by you who has transcended all religions. You tell us now…Is the crime committed by our prince so grave in nature that they are going to punish him with death?"

"The prince Dara Shiko is the eldest prince of this Mughal Empire. He is the eldest son of emperor Shahjahan who had won many wars leading an army of fifty thousand men and a cavalry of forty thousand horses. As a rule the eldest son of the king has to come to power. It doesn't matter much even if such thing is not honoured. Let the younger son Aunrangazeb appropriate the crown for himself. But what is the need to falsely accuse the prince Dara Shiko as Kafir, an enemy of Allah, and produce him in front of people ignominiously and get him awarded with death penalty? It doesn't fit any standard of ethics. Does it?"

"The very thinking that the life of a noble man, who showed the way to live a peaceful life beyond one's religion, is going to be taken away tomorrow, indeed, shakes our conscience. Please do something Guru" they beseeched Sarmad guru. Some of them in the crowd bawled out, vented out their frustration. Sitting in the middle of the crowd, I could see the love and affection people of Delhi had for their prince Dara Shiko. With my heart full of agony, I spoke in front of them. The multitude of people hailed every word I spoke with ferocious outcry.

"Is our prince Dara Shiko punished for comparing the Hinduism with Islam? Or is he treated as the enemy of god for he had compared five magnificent attributes commonly known as '*Ars e Azam*' comprising sky, wind, body, water and universe with the five elements mentioned in Hindu scriptures denoting the same? The God of creation, Lord Brahma is known in Islam as Holy Jibreil, the god of protection Lord Vishnu in Hinduism is known as the holy Micheal in Islam, and the god of destruction Lord Shiva is known as holy Israbil in Islam. Do these comparisons deserve death penalty given to Dara Shiko?"

"Is the comparison of *Sathyam, Sivam Sundaram* in Hindu philosophy with Islam's profound philosophies of *Al huq* (He is the truth), *Jabbar* and *Jameel* having similar resonance, often employed by Sufi saints, a big crime?"

"The Ulemas are convinced that they would be able to kill Dara Shiko, who has already been sitting in the hearts of people as their king, only if they pick up a weapon called religion. Don't they?"

The crowd grew agitated more as I continued my speech. There were some Ulemas in the crowd. My anger towards Mullahs grew intense.

"It is the duty of Sufis to find out the almighty god in the souls trapped in the body we cherish most. But it is the foolishness of some Mullahs that tries to find out the god almighty in the empty space of sky. I recited Rubhaiyat verse as I continued my tirade against Mullahs.

"The one is who aware of truth about god

Is bigger than the heaven.

Mullah says

Ahmad went to the heaven

I, Sarmad, say

It was the heaven that had come to Ahmad"

Some Ulemas in the crowd got angry with me for my speech and walked out. I was giving a last and definitive talk on death punishment given to Dara Shiko.

"The blood shed for the sake of love

Will never go waste"

The people ran fast to the place where Dara Shiko had been kept isolated. The streets of Delhi bore gory sight of violence everywhere. It took long time for me to sleep. During that dreaded night, I needed the warmth of passionate love from my handsome Abhay Chand. We became one, forgetting ourselves.

I slept after a prolonged distressing struggle in my heart.

Abhay Chand- Delhi- Later part of seventeenth century

The procession in which Dara Shiko would be exposed to public insult did start. People gathered on the streets of Delhi and thunderous yells "Hail the Prince Dara Shiko" were reverberating every corner of the city.

I was standing in the crowd incognito. A man from the crowd mumbled into my ears, "Here is Dara Shiko. The prince who was defeated by his brother Aurangazeb. After defeating him, if he wants to butcher his brother, he can do it within the walls of this fort. Can't he? Why to parade him in this unnecessary procession?"

Another man standing near replied to him, "Friend, there is a reason behind it. Aurangazeb has arranged this procession as he wants the people of Delhi to see for themselves that the man he is going to execute is none other than the real Dara Shiko. If he doesn't do it, tomorrow someone would appear suddenly and declare himself Dara Shiko, claim still being alive and instigate people in impersonation to go against Aurangazeb. That is why this procession"

I thought what all this man, Aurangazeb was actually capable of. My heart sank in despair.

The procession of public insult had just begun. Dara Shiko was tied on a weak elephant with a chain. On the side of elephant, was found the younger son of Dara Shiko tied up. What a barbaric act it was! The one who was sitting behind Dara Shiko on the elephant was Aurangazeb's slave, Nasser Begh. His hand was wielding a big sword to kill Dara Shiko.

Behind the elephant, Bhagadur Khan, the army commander of Malik Jwan who had betrayed Dara Shiko for Aurangazeb was coming astride horse. Some from the crowd shouted seeing Malik Jwan's army commander. They shouted "Down with the traitor Malik Jwan. Down with his traitor commander". Some of them threw stones at them. Aurangazeb's soldier coming on a horse read the order of Aurangazeb aloud.

"The people of Delhi, do you know why this man Dara Shiko is going to be killed? This Dara Shiko is an atheist. He is against Allah and His messenger Prophet Muhammad. The Mughal Empire will no more tolerate such acts of *Kafirs.* So it becomes essential to execute such an atheist so as to establish the holy messages uttered by the messenger in this world, and guard the guidelines of the Shariyat laws."

People grew agitated hearing that announcement. "It is nothing but a blatant act of felony in the name of religion to hide your heinous designs to kill him in the game of usurping power." Someone screamed. Aurangazeb's soldiers had an extremely tough time to control the mob frenzy.

Some of the men in the crowd grew furious, came in groups and murdered the men of Bhagadur Khan. The fury of people had now turned into a bloody violence. Marching past all these violence, the procession reached the altar where Dara Shiko was scheduled to be executed.

.....

Here lay on the ground the chopped heads and torsos of Dara Shiko and his younger son. The people cried their hearts out, dejectedly. One among the crowd declared, "Aurangazeb could kill only the mortal remains of Dara Shiko. He can't kill Dara Shiko's religious tolerance, his skills in writing poetry, his broad knowledge on religions, and his outstanding paintings. Auragazeb can never destroy these immortal things of Dara Shiko".

Another man shouted back.

"Aurangazeb has been born just to kill people. The number of enemies waiting to be executed in his hands will get long till get gets the throne. First it was his father Shahjahan, Next it was his own younger brother and then his younger sister."

"Apart from all these killings, Auarangazeb has been planning to kill his biggest enemy. It is our beloved guru Sarmad Kashani, the closest friend of Dara Shiko, who was commanding immense love from the people of Delhi."

I felt every pulse of my body turn lifeless all of a sudden when I heard those words. *"My beloved mama would be murdered"* – I stood stunned, unable to digest these tormenting words. *'Aurangazeb can go to any extent to do this. A simple fact of us being homosexuals is sufficient for him to execute my mama. The people of Delhi who had transcended religions are not against same sex relations. Had they thought it wrong, they wouldn't have gathered in such large numbers in front of Jumma masjid every day to have a glimpse of my mama. Would they?*

Nude Saint Sarmad Kashani, Abhay Chand and his other disciples.

"So Aurangazeb would definitely need a reason to murder him. O! God! Will these murderers slaughter my mama? Would my love meet its death? No…No…never it should happen."

I paced fast to my mama's residence.

The sentence found on the tomb of Sarmad guru.

Sarmad Kashani- Delhi- later part of Seventeenth century

"The haji is looking for the words in the holy Quran

He preaches everyone

Till his mouth aches

If his heart doesn't drench in love

Would there be any use being a teacher to others?

A Hindu Sadhu colours his cloths in saffron

But he doesn't know the colour of love

If then does it matter

Whether his dress is white or is made of stone?"

Abhay Chand was singing this song of Saint Kabhir Das in ghazal with his honey laden voice. The crowd that had thronged to visit me was sitting spell bound listening to his song. My mind, unable to relish his melody, kept thinking of the gory incidents that had been orchestrated in Delhi. The mighty king of this Mughal Empire Shahjahan was in jail. He kept telling everyone that his eldest son Dara Shiko would ascend the throne after him. Being a king, Shahjahan wasn't even aware that his eldest son Dara Shiko had been murdered by his younger son Aurangazeb. A warden of the jail in which Shahjahan was kept gave Shahjahan a parcel telling him that his son Aurangazeb had sent him a gift.

The king opened the parcel happily only to see the severed head of his son Dara Shiko. Seeing his son's chopped head, the king fell unconscious never to get up again. He had then been bed ridden till now. It was reported that Aurangazeb, the ruthless man had finished off not only Dara Shiko but all his brothers and other relatives who stood on his way opposing his ascendance to power. Countless murders of Sikhs, Hindus and Sufis! With his lunatic way conducting polity mixed up with religion, Auarangazeb had literally become a maddened elephant.

'I was his next target of murder. I was teaching people religious harmony that everyone is same, there is only one god, He is Allah, and He is Lord Ram. If Aurangazeb could succeed in murdering me who holds a permanent place in the hearts of people of Delhi, then there would be no one left out to question that tyrant's religious fundamentalism. In order to ensure his tyrannical ways, Aurangazeb would go to any extent to

kill anyone. Nothing would change with the expression of my compunctions anyway.' As though having understood what I was thinking, Abhay Chand sang another verse of Kabhir Das in ghazal.

"Keep the scandaliser beside you

Make a beautiful hut for him in your garden

It is he who would cleanse all your sins without using

cleanser and water."

What a wonderful poem it was! Saint Kabhir Das was also a proponent of Hindu-Muslim unity like me and Prince Dara Shiko. If saint Kabhir Das could compose a verse like this predicting impending dangers from enemies, the dangers I faced were nothing in front of it. Were they?

'I am seeing the sycophants of mullahs and henchmen of Ulemas sitting in the front in the crowd to pick up a slip of tongue from my speech. As said by saint Kabhir Das I have been keeping enemies near to me. One day I may also be slain. I am ready for anything.'

Abhay Chand- Delhi- later part of Seventeenth Century

I couldn't get good sleep during nights these days. During day, the life had got miserable, without peace of mind. The fear of losing my beloved mama had been tormenting me every day, every second.

Our love which had been melting our souls for the last twenty years, our love which grew ridiculing religious bigotry, our love which flourished nude beyond petty appearances and ornaments was now hanging for its survival at the tip of Aurangazeb's sword.

Earlier, mama used to assuage my woes whenever I was sad. Sometimes he would pinch my waist, sometime he would lovingly pat my butts, and sometimes he would pamper me carrying me on his chest. But none of these is happening now. Mama might be thinking that Abhay Chand must learn to live his life alone without him. The atrocities of Aurangazeb orchestrated in the name of religion were on rise day after day. At the same time, Mama's lectures on religious harmony, his teachings on oneness of god and one humanity were also growing popular among the people of Delhi.

Having learnt the increasing influence of Mama through his spies, one day Aurangazeb appeared in front of Mama, suddenly. It seemed that he had suddenly decided to meet mama when he went Jumma Masjid for prayer. I ran away from the spot fearing his presence and watched on silently what was happening.

Aurangazeb gestured to his guards to stand at a distance and approached Mama. His eyes emitted contempt.

"Hei Fakir, you had told these people that eldest Dara Shiko only would ascend the throne. Hadn't you? Now see for yourself what had happened." Mama remained undisturbed by Aurangazeb's thunderous voice. He replied with all his composure.

"I said that Dara Shiko would get the throne of God and he got it"

"This is just an escaping reply" Aurangazeb laughed again throwing his contemptuous eyes over Mama's nude body.

"Hei fakir, aren't you shamed of roaming nude? Why do you roam nude against the rules of the Shariyat?" his authoritative question got me damn intimidated. But mama remained very quiet, unperturbed and didn't show any sign of fear. Smiling at him, Mama recited a rubhaiyat verse.

"Allah has given clothes to sinners

To hide their sins.

He has given nudity

To the pure souls."

Aurangazeb's anger grew many folds with mama's reply. His furious stumping on ground with his legs attested his anger.

"You stupid fakir, I live by the Shariyat laws. Is it wrong?" Aurangazeb yelled at Mama. Yet Mama remained unmoved and spoke calmly.

"King Alamgir, I appreciate that you live by the Shariyat laws. But I oppose the way you kill people who don't like to live by the Shariyat laws". Though Aurangazeb's anger grew more, he didn't prefer show it in words and rather stared at mama with his derisive eyes.

"You useless fakir, you are keeping a rug near you. Can I cover your nude body with that rug?" Aurangazeb sneered.

Mama didn't utter anything, kept smiling.

Aurangazeb bent down, removed the rug and jumped off in disbelief. "aahhhhhh..."

He stood at a distance, visibly shocked, and looked askance at what he saw inside the rug. He couldn't believe what he had just seen under the rug. He went near to the rug again and again, removed it and saw again and stood stupefied in total shock.

As he was not sure what he had seen, he ordered some of his guards to see under the rug. They also yelled in shock seeing it and ran away from it.

Under the rug, were there the severed head and headless torso of Aurangazeb's elder brother Dara Shiko. Along with it, there were many lifeless corpses without heads. Those headless bodies belonged to the men who had been butchered by Aurangazeb out of his lunatic religious bigotry and mad rage to seize the throne. Sarmad Kashani, my beloved mama, smiled at Aurangazeb and told,

"What should I hide with this rug?

Your sins?

Or my nudity?"

Aurangazeb was at the peak of anger as he couldn't bear the insulting talk from Sarmad guru and he shrieked in high pitch, "Youuu…naked fakir…who the hell are you knowing this magic? Are you a conjurer?"

Mama glanced at Aurangazeb silently for some time. His face grew brightened up suddenly. In that state of nothingness, he recited a rubhaiyat song.

"I am the king of kings

O Sheik…I don't have the nudity you have in you.

Though I am a spiritual mad

My attention would never go astray out of petty interests.

Truly I am atheist anyway.

I would worship idols

But I am not a complete theist either

Though I visit mosques

I am not a pious Muslim.

I am just a follower of the truth of god

I am a guard to the path leading to Him

I am Jews guru, an atheist, not a Muslim

I am just a naked fakir"

Mama's followers who had assembled there erupted in joy at this reply. Some of them paid their regards and some of them touched his phallus with their hands reverently and then gently rubbed their eyes with those hands. Hell-shocked, Aurangazeb couldn't utter anymore. Fuming, he left the place at once along with his guards.

Mama was now smiling but I was greatly petrified even to think what would happen next.

Sarmad Kashani- Delhi- later part of seventeenth century

It had been a couple of months since Aurangazeb came to our residence. There were no changes in me but the city of Delhi had witnessed innumerable changes. The city which used to be very quiet earlier had now turned into a place witnessing violence every day due to the fanatic tyrant called Aurangazeb.

It was reported that Aurangazeb had been discussing with his officials to reintroduce Jizya tax on non-muslims in accordance with the Shariyat laws. What an atrocious act it was! This Jizya tax, which was abolished by the Emperor

Akbar who had equal respect for all religions, was going to be introduced again by Auragazeb.

'Before god, every human being is his child. Only humans can distinguish among themselves as Hindus, Muslins, Sikhs and Jews. But god would never does such discrimination among his children. How could one, who treats Muslims favourably on one hand and ill-treats non-Muslims on other hand, be a God of everyone? And, how could the rules framed by such a god be the true rules for everyone?'

'Whether is it I who has been insulting god with my nudity or is it Aurangazeb who has been insulting god by his differential attitude to divide people?'

As soon as the news of reintroduction of Jizya tax spread across the city, the people of Delhi thronged in crowds to meet me. An increasing crowd day by day. *'Now I have been forced to talk politics apart from spirituality. Even today I am addressing the people of Delhi. My talk is a mixture of politics and spirituality.'* I watched the crowd that had assembled before me. That day, Aurangazeb's elder daughter Zebunnisa was also sitting in the crowd.

She was a pearl born in an oyster's shell. She could appreciate the profoundness of truth found in Sufism. Even at the age of seven she could memorise the holy Quran to earn the title Hafisa. Aurangazeb who once used to be very proud and fond of his seven year old daughter who earned a big title had now started slowly disliking her due to her liberal attitude towards religions.

It was very unfortunate that Aurangazeb who knew nothing about the importance of humanity happened to be a father of a girl who held humanity in high regard than religions.

She was waiting till I completed my lecture. Once it was over, she came to meet me in private and paid her obeisance.

"You always have my blessing dear daughter. I have been reading the verses you send me regularly. You are a wonderful human being who could bring out the profoundness of Allah in beautiful words."

She smiled at me, very elegantly. "My guru's words of praise makes me feel shy. How would I write those verses? The lessons I have learnt from learned men like you, the way you showed a new way of approaching God, Allah are the source of my inspiration to write spiritual poems" Zebunnisa told, and bowed her head in reverence. I blessed her once again. Our conversation turned to other direction. "Guruji, do you remember one day you had kept some huts made of clay on the main roads of Delhi?

"Yes dear daughter, I do remember. You asked me to sell you one of those huts"

Zebunnisa grinned. It's true. You asked me to give you some tobacco as price of it before selling it to me. I gave you some tobacco and took that hut to my palace"

"Yes dear daughter, I remember I sold it after inscribing your name 'Zebunnisa' on that clay hut"

Zebunnisa resumed, "My father Aurangazeb didn't know that I had bought that clay hut from you. My father told me he had a dream that night. In that dream, my father Aurangazeb was in the heaven. While taking a stroll around the heaven he happened to come across a magnificent, beautiful bungalow standing in front of him. Smitten by its grand beauty, he ventured to get into it. But he was denied entry by some unseen force obstructing him. He was incensed at it and wanted to know who owned that bungalow. He read the name inscribed on the bungalow walls. It carried my name Zebunnisa inscribed on it"

Her story got me amused. "Ok..then what happened? I teased her to go ahead.

"My father told me that he had to come to meet me as he saw my name in his dream. This forced me to tell him the story behind the purchase of clay hut from you"

At once he heard your name from my mouth he grew terribly furious, and shouted at me, "He is a naked cunning magician. If you get friendly with that naked fakir, your dreams will only be like this. If only I kill him, the people of Delhi will mend their ways."

I was damn petrified at his words, Master" she said.

I laughed at her face that went pale. "Don't worry my dear daughter. True heaven is in our heart. Men like Aurangazeb who believe in religious codes would see heaven only in dreams." Zebunnisa intervened and told, "No matter what it is...you please be careful. Your life is in danger, Master"

"I know dear daughter" I smiled at her, poised. Zebunnisa bid me adieu and left.

Her words of warning didn't leave any impact on me. I remained calm as usual. But it was Abhay Chand who was extremely worried about my life, tormenting his body and health.

Seeing him in distress, I told him one day, "Abhay Chand, I really appreciate your devotion for me. The love you shower on me like a wife doing on her husband leaves me amazed."

Without replying to my observations, Abhay Chand sobbed bitterly. Comforting him, I kissed him.

"My dear Abhay Chand, if an elephant becomes mad, there are possibilities that its mahout who controls it with his goad might become its first kill. So, if religions grow mad, it is quite possible that the persons like me who control it with our teaching of religious harmony might fall its first kills. If it is true that destiny has united us together for last twenty years, you must believe that the same destiny would separate us too"

I cuddled his trembling body. Our sexual union that night was something extraordinary we had never experienced so far. I knew the reason behind it- it was going to be our last coital pleasure.

When I rose in the morning next day, I saw a soldier from Aurangazeb standing outside my house.

"The quasi judge has ordered to bring you to the court for enquiry. Come with me now" he said. I was fully aware what was waiting to be unfolded. I and Abhay Chand followed that soldier.

Abhay Chand- Delhi- later part of seventeenth century

"After that incident you did see yourself how my mama was brutally slaughtered yesterday. Didn't you? I don't have anything more to say. Do I?" I said to that Sufi man sitting beside me.

On the banks of river Yamuna, I and my mama's spirit narrated our love story to the Sufi sitting in front of us.

My mama's spirit left me now. I cried helplessly. The misery I was undergoing made me cry desolately. The Sufi saint listening to my story was left helpless not knowing how to comfort me.

"Brother Abhay Chand, this world might forget your love story one day. But one day the same sex relations would be recognised. The time is not too far. That day, this story of deep love would also emerge. The parochial circle of religions would get sunk in the broader circle of humanity. The fame of Sarmad Kashani who conceived humanity beyond petty religious narrow mindedness, would spread all over the world. Till this Jumma Masjid stands here in Delhi, till that tomb of Hara Bhare stands there, this world would keep coming there to receive the blessings of Sarmad Kashani buried under it. Don't worry dear brother. I take leave"

The Sufi saint puffed on *Ganja* to douse the fire of depression burning in his heart. Then, the pure Sufi heart bid me farewell and left.

I remained severely depressed, without peace in mind. The scene of my mama being butchered came through my mind again and again.

Yesterday in the Jumma Masjid, the executioner, with his sword raised above head spoke, "Sarmad, the criminal, you need not see your head when it is chopped off. Let me cover your head with a wrap. What do you say?"

Sarmad mama looked at the executioner holding his sword above his head, with unflustered eyes, and told him, "You may sever my head without covering it with clothe". He sang a rubhaiyat song even at the time his head waiting for sword on the altar.

"This sword of this friend became naked.

God has come in impersonation to gift me death

I accept it whole heartedly.

O god! This is the sacrifice of your ardent devotee.

Once I lose my head, my story will come to an end.

The trouble of being a head ache

Will disappear today"

The quasi judge became enraged at Mama's verse. He roared, "You arrogant atheist, it is not yet over. Utter the entire Kalima Tayyiba now. Just utter Allah is the only god. I will let you go"

Mama, nonchalantly, sang another Rubhaiyat verse.

"I am in the undesirable quest for reaching omnipotent god.

I am void of inner strength in my search for god.

If I say Kalima with this half faith

I will then become a liar."

The sword descended with a swift swing. Unable to see that gory scene, I fell unconscious, exasperatingly yelling out.

I was horribly troubled by the scene of murder. *'What an atrocity! What an atrocity! Just because my mama was adamant in not telling entire Kalima Tayyiba he was killed.'*

A sudden surge of fury did built in me. My face bore the expression of unbridled anger. I shouted with all my might that shook the entire stretch of the river Yamana.

"*La ilaha illallahu muhammadur rasulullah... La ilaha illallahu muhammadur rasulullah...La ilaha illallahu muhammadur rasulullah*" I got into the river Yamuna shouting the entire Kalima Tayyiba aloud.

I was playing my Ektara, hysterically, as I walked deep into the water. The strings of my Ektara broke within minutes. I was moving further into the river.

"You fool...Aurangazeb, I have uttered the entire Kalima Tayyiba which my mama refused to. Have you heard the entire Kalima uttered by me, Abhay Chand, a Hindu? Just because I uttered Allah is the only god, would Lord Narayana who I worship every day get me beheaded? If he does it, would he be a god? Lord Vishnu and Allah are one and the same. Lord Ram and Rahim are one and the same. I curse you that you would die without even understanding this philosophy. You dupe Aurangazeb, you will never be absolved of your sins of separating my mama from me. You, a diabolic, who doesn't know what relationship is all about, a day will come you will face the ignominy of being hated by your own sons and daughters. The day will come you will be imprisoned and killed by your own most pampered daughter Zebunnisa. As all your heirs standing against you, the day will come you would become mad and die like an orphan. While praising your lord Allah every time, you never have any compunction to kill people at your whims when it comes to usurping throne. Is it the righteousness Allah had taught you? You are an ignoramus who never understands that it is love and compassion that Allah represents. You will die such a humiliating death repenting your ending days. The time will come all Marathas, Sikhs, Rajasthanis and others from various religions of Hindustan would wage a war against your regime. You will become a pauper spending huge amount of money on your army to face these people in war. Don't forget one thing Aurangazeb. Be it a Hindu, or a Muslim, whoever it may be, if he is drunk with religious bigotry, this Hindustan will never allow him to live long because religious extremism is the biggest enemy of Hindustan. Whenever religious extremism raises its ugly head, Hindustan will see a surge of force to decimate it. No matter who speaks of religious extremism, be it Hindu or Muslim. Hindustan won't sleep till all such men are wiped out from its soil. In Hindustan, one day Jainism would come up to rule, another day Buddhism, another day Islam and Christianity. But it doesn't matter which religion it is, those who rule in the name of religious fundamentalism will perish for sure. This has been the history of Hindustan. So, you will also perish one day"

"You are a man having no faith in humans! The time will come you will spend sleepless nights at different places, being hopeless, fearing that some unknown enemy would kill you. You will die a death losing all your hope and peace"

"Let the river Yamuna where many religions were nurtured stand as witness to my curse. Let the Taj Mahal which sings the sanctity of love on the banks of Yamuna River stand as witness to my curse. Let the Jumma masjid where my mama is sleeping stand as witness to my curse"

"The day will come the world would stop treating same sex a sin and recognise it as a sacred one. The day will come the world would celebrate our same sex relations buried under Hare Bhare tomb in front of Jumma Masjid. I pledge this on my sacred love; I pledge this on my holy seeds"

I was descending deep into the waters of the river Yamuna.

Ended

3
Lunar Dynasty

King Sudyumna

I shot my last arrow from my quiver. This time too, the arrow shot piercing through the air missed its target, and the deer escaped. There were no arrows left in my quiver for my further attempts of shooting.

As a ruler of Palika Kingdom, I remained startled at my ability. *'Although being a son of Manu, the first ever king of human race, and an accomplished archer in hitting the target without fail, I haven't been able to kill a small deer. What an insult!'*

In the thick of a forest, as I was chasing a deer which sprinted faster than wind for its life, I was lost in the jungle, driven far away from my soldiers. As I was extremely tired of running for a long distance, I sat down on the ground. It was when a Yakshini appeared before me and bowed her head in reverence.

"My lord, first of all, I seek your forgiveness for diverting your attention taking the form of a deer and make you feel fatigued." I didn't get cooled down even after seeing Yakshini stand politely beseeching forgiveness.

"When you were on your way hunting, I and my dear husband Yakshan were together taking the form of deer. We were afraid of being killed by your arrows" told Yakshini, still quivering as she talked. "Since my husband is sick, he can't hide for life like me. In order to save his life, I got your attention diverted from us, and sped in the form of deer. Lord, I seek your pardon for making you feel very tired"

Yakshini disappeared after seeking pardon from me.

Sitting on the ground, I looked around the jungle. Very near to me, some peahens were picking grains from the thickly grown grass bed. I looked for peacocks in that pride. To my dismay, I couldn't find even a single peacock amidst those peahens with no plumage.

Some big sized wild hens were fighting with each other crowing feverishly. There too, I couldn't find any wild rooster.

"How's that possible?" I didn't understand.

I rose, walked slowly and saw some cows grazing but there was no a bull among those cows. I was doubly surprised at it.

I looked up to the trees, there were female parrots, female cuckoos but no sign of male members of species. It was something amazing.

For a long time, I was walking through that thick jungle where trees were found grown tall. While walking, my eyes were on search for signs of any males. There was nothing known as masculinity. It was femininity that ruled everywhere.

Trees were feminine, flowers were feminine, the beetles hovering over the flowers were feminine, everywhere feminine and in all it is feminine. *'Am I the only male there?'*

As I was tired of walking a long distance, I felt my tongue dried up. When I was walking aimless, thirsty with tongue dried up, I saw a pond at a calling distance.

I walked towards the pond eagerly. But with the legs which were dead tired, I could only trudge slowly. I almost reached the pond. It was that time I saw a beautiful damsel in grey colour. She was sitting in the water where it wasn't deep, stretching out her legs. She was half-naked without covering her breasts. The small piece of cloth she had tied below her waist slid off at times and exposed her hidden grey beauty a bit liberally.

Due to thick growth of tall trees around it, and wild creepers spread across, that beautiful pond lay in dark without receiving much of sun light. Yet, that grey damsel's beauty was shining even in the darkness. Hiding myself behind wild bushes grown around the pond, I was relishing the beauty of her body without batting my eyes.

In my private chambers in Palika kingdom, I had had relished dark and pink colour breasts. This was the first time in my life I got to see grey colour breasts. Both those grey breasts were rounded, fleshy and erect like wood apple. Just below those wood apples, was found a beautiful round naval resembling a mild dent made by middle finger in the ball of sweetened flour used for lighting a wick while worshipping god.

She scooped out some water from the pond in her palms and bathed her grey breasts. The cold water which flew down her breasts entered her naval area. The water staying up in her naval reminded me of water flowing down from snow-capped mountains, falling as water falls filling that pond. It roused my wild, passionate fantasies.

The water filled her naval was too chill for her to bear. She rose from the water with a quivering hiss and twisted her waist uncomfortably due to chillness. Tuned with the twist of her waist, her two fully rounded grey buttocks too swung from side to side rhythmically. My manhood kept tamed till now found its way and got unleashed. I thought of going near to her. But another surprise awaited there for me.

The grey beauty came out of pond and it seemed she wasn't embarrassed at seeing her own nakedness. Someone near gave out a brief chuckle at seeing her naked body.

'*O! There is another woman around here*" my heart grew chill. I hid myself fully behind thick bushes, and started watching them.

"Why are you laughing?" asked the grey beauty as she went near to her friend. The other woman was also equally beautiful. But she had her cloths on after bath.

"You are a naked grey beauty" the woman complimented and hugged the grey beauty tightly. The grey beauty reciprocated her friend's tight hug and crushed her breasts against her friend's breasts. Both the beautiful women showered kisses on each other's lips. My body went limp, grew terribly hot as I saw them flirting with kisses.

The grey beauty kneaded the buttocks of the yellow beauty. I stood astounded at seeing them cuddling with elegant moves akin to that of two snakes curling on each other. I haven't seen two women having sex so far. As long as I kept watching their sexual act, my passionate longing indeed grew more never to be subsided. Mustering some courage, I made a mild sound by clearing my throat.

The yellow beauty under the complete intoxication of sex, was not in a state to give her ears to the sound I made. But the grey beauty who had stolen my heart could identify my presence there. Her face carried such an expression of contempt as if she had known who I was and where I had come from.

"You…stupid king Sudyumna, You silly king…what the heck of a nonsense is this?"- I was shattered at the grey beauty's thunderous voice of anger. It…it was not voice of a woman. It was a resplendent male voice coming out of a female body. It was quite unexpected.

The grey beauty became furious, her eyes grew red. Slowly she was becoming a male. The yellow beauty also changed into her original form, Parvathi. I howled at in sheer shock. The one standing in front of me was not that grey colour woman. It was my lord Shiva who bore grey hue on his body. The one standing beside Him was his wife, Parvathi.

"Om…Nama Shivaya…Om…Nama Parvathi Saranam…O! My mother! O! My father" I prostrated onto the ground, on their feet.

Lord Shiva'a anger hadn't come down. "You petty soul Sudyumna, as my wife desired, I had converted this whole forest into feminine one and named it 'Shravanavanam'. As there is no presence of any males here, I became a female and was having sex with her. But, not being aware of my intention, you just entered this forest and defiled the purity of our relationship. This Shravanavanam has also got spoiled with your presence"- the severity of his words didn't diminish.

"My lord…please forgive me" I kneeled before him and beseeched his pardon. But the Lord still roared in anger.

"You…a scoundrel who lusted after the nudity of your lord. Let you be a woman henceforth" he threw a curse upon me. I cried helplessly receiving the curse of Lord Shankar.

I strode fast to Mother Parvathi. "O! My mother. There is no such thing you aren't aware of. It is a mistake I committed unknowingly due to my destiny and is it right to give me such a big punishment for this inadvertent mistake, mother? Please do something so that I can get redeemed of it" I grasped Parvathi's legs and begged.

The Mother grew softened. She glanced at her husband, Lord Shiva with her flower-like eyes caressingly.

"My Lord! You are the one who told this world that men and women are equal. There is no such thing in this world you are unaware of. But I feel it is my duty to remind you of that. This man Sudyumna had actually been a female when he was born" Lord Shiva was patiently listening to her words. The goddess continued.

"The first king of human race, Manu was the father of this Sudyumna who is standing in front. His mother's name was Sharddha. Since they were childless for a long time, Manu and his wife Shraddha went to Agasthiya rishi for the boon of getting a baby. Agasthiya rishi conducted a Yagna and prayed to God Mithra and God Varuna. While praying to these gods, Manu and Shraddha wrongly chanted the mantras which Agasthiya had taught them. This resulted in god Mithra and God Varuna blessing the couple with a female baby instead of a male baby. The couple was sad as their eldest child happened to be a female baby. They prayed to Mithra and Varuna once again for a male baby. Both the gods were considerate seeing the couple's penance and offered them a boon. The boon bestowed by these two gods changed the sex of the baby from female to male. The happy couple named the child Sudyumna and made him the king of Palika kingdom."

Goddess Parvathi gasped as was telling the story of my birth, the story of a man named as Sudyumna. Lord Shiva remained silent as if waiting for her to blurt out more. Parvathi resumed her talk.

"When the story of his birth has such a heart breaking backdrop, I expect my lord to realise that his curse upon this poor fellow to become a woman would hurt his parents so much who did everything to have a male baby" She paused speaking and looked up to her husband. Lord Shiva didn't show any sign of pity even after the continuous coaxing of Mother Parvathi. The lord was not ready to forgive me for having enjoyed the complete nakedness of His grey body.

It was Mother Goddess who became soft-hearted at seeing my condition and started blessing me.

"Sudyumna, I pity you for what all happened. But you cannot be fully absolved of Lord Shiva's curse that had descended upon you" Goddess Uma Devi continued. "The Lord's curse will have its effect on you ever. It can't be reverted. Yet, I pity you for your misery. So, you don't have to live as woman throughout your life as you were cursed. Instead, you can live as a woman for a month and as a man for next month all through your life"

I was listening to *Her* words with a devotional attentiveness and fear in heart. The Mother Goddess continued, when you live as a man, you would be known as Sudyumna and Ila when you live as a woman. Do remember one thing. During the month you live as a man, you will forget your life as a woman during the preceding month. Similarly, when you live as a woman you will forget your life as a man. You may go now"

Watching the softness in His wife's voice, Artha Nareeswara gave out a pejorative sneer. I once again fell flat on the ground and paid my obeisance to the Lord and Mother Goddess. The Lord took the form of grey colour woman and went near to Mother Goddess coquettishly.

I completely lost my interest to relish the beauty of grey colour woman. I took to my heels to get out of the Shravanavanam as soon as possible. While I was running away from that forest, I saw me changing into a beautiful woman, Ila.

I could trace out my soldiers who I had lost in the forest. But as I didn't like to go back to my country in the form of a woman, I stayed up in the forest and roamed. Even after lord Shiva and Parvathi had left for their abode in the Mount Kailash, I was still roaming in the forest.

God Budha

"Pringu kaliga shyam

Rubena prathimam butham

Soumyam Soumya kunobetham

Tham budham pranamam yaham"

--'Though I am not a saint who renounced everything, this world would praise me as God Budha who knows how to control all his five elements'-.

After I became aware of the truth behind my birth, I couldn't help feeling pity about myself. An unendurable sadness in life had left in my heart a scar that never got healed. I was in desperate need of peace of mind now.

I came to this Shravanavanam in search of mental peace. I entered Shravanavanam where lord Shiva and Goddess Parvathi made love before leaving that place, for the first time. As the lord Shiva and goddess Parvathi had already left for their abode in the Mount Kailash, the forest lay very calm.

I sat on the banks of the beautiful pond there. My thoughts went back to reflecting the story behind my birth. My father Soman alias Chandran became extremely powerful by conducting so many yagnas. As he grew powerful day by day, he became arrogant also simultaneously. It was at that time, he happened to meet my step father Brahaspathi during one of his Yagnas along with Brahspathi's wife Tara, my mother. As Chandran was smitten by Tara's beauty, another man's wife, he somehow wooed her and developed sexual relationship with her well before the yagnas were over. Tara, as she stayed with Chandran, became pregnant too.

Having lost his wife to another man, Brahaspathi became very angry and came with a large army to attack Chandran. This matter went to Lord Brahma who, in turn, mediated between Brahaspathi and Chandran. Tara returned to Brahaspathi. When she returned home, she was carrying me in her womb.

My step father Brahaspathi became almost mentally wrecked seeing his wife, Tara carrying Chandran's baby in her womb. However, he was magnanimous enough to treat me as his own son even though I was born out of an illicit relationship of my mother with Chandran. During my formative years, I wasn't aware of this fact…but after becoming a grown up man…when I came to know about the betrayal of my biological father Chandran to Brahaspathi, I was totally shattered. I came to this Shravanavanam so as to find some solace due to my unbearable mental agony.

I sat on meditation. My mind became calm and began travelling in a world of peace. It was all for a very short time as I got disturbed by the burbling sound in water. Someone might be drinking water….There…There….I found a beautiful damsel drinking water from the pond. When she was drinking water bending down, I saw her fully rounded beautiful breasts and her plumb behinds. My heart went weak seeing those assets. I, known for my ability to control the five elements, was now standing completely oblivious of my existence before the beauty of that woman.

My masculinity was aroused.

"Who could it be?" with the help of my clairvoyance I could see who she was. I understood the miserable story behind her.

'Due to the curse of Lord Shiva, she will be a woman with the name Ila this month and will become a man Sudyumna next month'.

I looked at Ila intently. *'What a beauty she is! I can do any damn thing just to own this splendid beauty. So what if she is a woman for a month, I reconciled myself. I can make love with her during this month. When she becomes a man next month, I can think of other ways to own her (him).'*

I strode slowly to her and told, "Ila, I am completely besotted with your beauty. Will you marry me?"

Ila glanced at me. She fell in love with my deific appeal. I grasped her tender hands and gently pulled them towards me.

That time I felt a group of people pressing my back with the tips of their spears. I turned back to see who they were. They were Ila's soldiers from Palika Kingdom. They were his devoted body guards who had pledged their allegiance to their royalty. They didn't leave Sudyumna even after he was cursed to become a woman.

I became angry and shouted at them, "Take your lances off"

But those body guards neither respected my anger nor took their lances off from my back.

"You silly idiots! You will all be eunuchs from today as you don't respect my words" I threw a curse at them. Following my curse, Ila's body guards became eunuchs, a gender in which neither would they be treated male nor female. I got ready to leave with my sweet heart, beautiful Ila.

One of the guards who became a eunuch spoke to me, "My lord, kindly pardon us for our mistakes. As we have become eunuchs, who would be available for us to have sex?"

I replied, calmly.

"Being a transgender is not something undignified. You mustn't forget that your king Sudyumna is a transgender himself"

Those soldiers were standing courteously, gazing at me as if expecting something from me. I resumed, "If your transgender king could get a partner like me, you would also get your partners soon. Wouldn't you? I bless you all to have appropriate partners in your life in future"

My blessing made them happy. They bid us farewell and left. Now I and Ila were left alone.

That night became one of the most pleasant nights in our life. Ila became pregnant that night. Next month is nearing and Ila would become a man. "How will I treat her as my wife next month?' I was overtly perplexed.

Ila and God Budha (Ila in female form)

Ila and God Budha (Ila in male form)

God Budha

The succeeding month arrived. Due to the curse of Lord Shiva, my wife Ila changed into a man, Sudyumna. As I couldn't do anything about it, we reconciled to live our life as per the divine command of god.

I entered Sudyumna's hut. Seeing me, he greeted me reverently, "O! God Budha, I am indeed blessed to have you in my hut" Sudyumna said.

I understood Sudyumna has completely forgotten his life in the preceding month as woman, Ila. "Be blessed Sudyumna. Are you alright here?" I asked him endearingly. Actually, my mind was full of Ila when I was looking at him intently.

"I am good my lord. But I couldn't still make out how did I land up in this forest? I am not aware where had those soldiers of Palika gone? "Sudyumna was visibly confused while replying.

I was afraid that my dearest Ila might leave that forest in the form of Sudyumna.

"Don't worry Sudyumna, on my way to this forest I also lost my army. So I would stay with you as your companion and you'd be my companion." I told, heaving a big sigh.

"As you wish my lord! I will remain blessed for having this opportunity to serve you" he suddenly fell on the ground unconscious as he was speaking.

I got stunned and lifted him anxiously, checked his pulse, *'O! Sudyumna is pregnant now. She fell unconscious due to her pregnancy. As a result of our pleasant days in the preceding month when he was a woman, he is now carrying my child.'*

I felt laughing- *'A man has become pregnant and carrying a child. It is all the mercy of King of Kailash, Lord Shiva. If it is destined by god, we have to accept it anyway'*. I went near to Sudyumna. I woke him up sprinkling water on his face.

He regained his consciousness but I didn't tell him about his pregnancy.

"I am hungry" Sudyumna said. I went to my hut and brought him some food to eat. After having food, he went out and picked out some unripe mangoes from Mango trees. I just watched him without saying anything to him.

'*My lovely Ila is now a man*'- I glanced at him intently- Same rounded face of my wife Ila, same beautiful eyes, and same chiselled lips which I tasted last month with only one noticeable difference- he had a moustache above his lips.

"Sudyumna, please come here" I called him out fondly. "Lord" he came near. As he came near, I kissed his lips. He was startled, pulled him away from me and threw an inscrutable smile at me.

"My lord, what is this? I have been thinking of making all the arrangements for the pursuit of your spiritual service. But you …."

"What do you mean by '*you*'? I teased him. Sudyumna continued. "If a man kisses another man, wouldn't that be awkward?"

Without immediately replying to his question, I remained silent for some time.

'*How would that be awkward Sudyumna? Lord Shiva's curse is on you, not on me. Even when you are a male, I think I have all right to treat you as my wife Ila. My lord Shiva and mother goddess Parvathi won't stop me doing it because that curse is only on you Sudyumna, not on me*' I told myself.

Sudyumna continued, "There is no such thing that you remain unaware including the Manusmiriti my father wrote. Don't you?" Sudyumna laughed aloud.

I also laughed aloud. Chapter eleven, Part 174- is it the one you want me to know? I prefer you say it for me"

Sudyumna smiled and then continued. "According to Manusmiriti written by my father a man has to eat *Panjakavaya* as a punishment for having sex with another man" Sudyumna paused. I continued.

"It means one has to eat Panjakavya, a combination of cow urine, cow dung, cow milk, cow ghee, and cow curd. Is that right? Anything more?" I asked.

Sudyumna mumbled into my ears, "After such a sexual union between same sex people, they shouldn't eat for a full day after that."

I also muttered into his ears, "I know…I know…then what?" I teased him further.

Sudyumna continued, 'then according to Chapter eleven, Part 175, one has to take bath with his cloth on."

"No issue in this. We can bathe. Anything more?"

Sudyumna looked at me absorbedly, amazed. He seemed to have understood what was going on in my mind. In my eyes, I could see only my wife Ila. Without uttering anything more, Sudyumna brought a wooden mat for sitting while conducting puja, a broad plate, incense burner, hand bell, a standing lamp, pot, jug, bowl, camphor, cow milk, ghee, *navadanya* (nine types of grains), turmeric, kumkum, banana leaves, and *Thamboolam* and kept them in front of me. Praising his sincerity in his assisting me in my spiritual pursuits, I completed my puja.

Night came, I couldn't come out of Ila's thought. I felt that I had to convince Sudyumnaa who was otherwise my Ila. I entered Sudyumna's hut and lay beside him. Feeling my hot breath crawling on his body, Sudyumna turned to me and said, "My lord, your wishes do define my existence"

"*Vikriti evam prakriti*". Anything that seems to contradict nature, are in a way a part of the very nature Sudyumna" I said.

I hugged my Ila, who was in the body of Sudyumna. He grinned silently. It was all for a very short time, he rose swiftly and sat. Hardly had he vomited with an awkward sound, I stretched out my hand to collect his vomit. Seeing his muck caused by pregnancy, I was alarmed. *'A man is vomiting due to pregnancy. My Ila, who is in a male body, will face humiliation and insults. Won't she? O! My lord! What sort of a test you have put both of us in? Om Namashivaya'*

I cried as my tears rolled down my cheeks. Sudyumna also cried. But it wasn't pregnancy which made him cry. He cried for the love I displayed for him. "My lord, your love is immeasurable. I understood it from the way you collected my vomit" he said.

We slept cuddling each other.

Ila

It had been five months since I became pregnant. *'Why would I get worried in life when I have my sweet husband Budha to look after me?'*. With my mind full of peace, I leaned against the shoulders of God Budha, who was known as Soumyan.

Lord Budha told me, "We have to conduct a bangle wearing ceremony in one of the waxing moon period soon. His tone showed that he wanted it urgently.

"Why my lord? Why this urgency? We can have that ceremony in the seventh month. Can't we?" I asked him lovingly.

"I want....I want..." he stammered. I looked at him questioningly.

"If we miss this waxing moon, we may not know what would happen in the next waxing moon." His voice was quivering mildly.

"It is alright, my lord. As you wish, we can have it" I remained silent.

I put on new cloths after a complete bath, my lord wore me a leaf bangle made of neem leaves on my hand and wild flowers be picked from the forest on my head. I was very happy.

"Stretch out your palm, Ila" Soumyan asked me lovingly and wore four bangles in one hand and five on another. My heart was brimmed with happiness.

"Our child should keep listening to the sounds of these bangles. The jingling of these bangles should keep our baby happy always. Will you do it, Ila for me?" when my lord Budha asked me, I bobbed head affirmatively.

"What are we going to name our baby, my lord?" I asked him eagerly.

Lord Budha looked at me with a beaming pride. "Ila... my beautiful wife, our son is going to be the first king of the Lunar Dynasty. He will be the first king of Kshatriya clan too. I am going to name him Pururuwas." My happiness knew no bounds as he continued speaking about our son.

I went to sleep peacefully.

Now, it was sixth month. Ila became Sudyumna again. He grew disorganised and explicitly confused at seeing the bangles in his hands. He looked at me, his lord.

"Sudyumna, these bangles are my gift of love. You should shake it near your stomach. Would you do it for the sake of your lord?"

Sudyumna laughed heartily. "I have worn bangles to many a women in my harem in my palace. Now, my lord is wearing bangles on my hands. What is happening here, my lord?"

I was unable to reply to his questions. I was caught up in a serious dilemma.

'How am I going to manage this situation?' My face fell. Sudyumna understood that I was undergoing some distress.

"My lord, don't worry. I understand something is bothering your mind which obstructs you telling me the truth. I won't ask any such complicated questions anymore"- promised Sudyumna. But I was worried about some other problem.

'If the child is born on ninth month, there will be no problem because Ila will be a woman that month and she will give birth to the baby through vulva. Or, even if she gives birth on the first day of eleventh month after completing tenth month, there will be no problem. But, when Sudyumna is a man in his tenth month, giving birth to the baby can be extremely risky. How will he give birth to the baby? Will he give birth tearing open his stomach? Or through his phallus?' I almost sank into despair and became insane at this very thought.

'Child birth through vulva is a very painful process by itself. Sudyumna is a man. If it happens to give birth to the child through his member, it will be extremely painful than vulva? Won't it?' I prayed to Lord Shiva and kneeled before him in my mind.

'My Lord, the king of Mount Kailsh, there is no limit to your tests of perseverance. My wife Ila, how many more days she has to bear this curse of living as a man and woman? How many more days will you give her such a life without peace. My Lord, enough of your tests', heart-broken, I cried inconsolably.

Now the tenth month had also come. I tried everything under my ability to ensure the baby would be born in the ninth month when Ila is a woman. But all went in vain. It was all His games. At the end of tenth month, Sudyumna developed labour pain. His pregnant stomach was very big and he couldn't walk either. His moans of excruciating pain troubled me a lot and my mind seemed to be losing its balance.

"*O! My Ila…my Ila…*" I kept whining in my heart.

Days and time were fast moving. The day my child was going see this world was also fast approaching and finally it arrived. I sank into thoughts as to what I should do to make Sudyumna give birth to the child easily. I took her clothes off and had her lain on her back.

"Don't worry Sudyumna, everything will be alright very soon." I stroked his head tenderly.

'My child will be born very soon'. I was watching Sudyumna, without a wink in my eyes.

I started chanting 'Siva...Shiva...Hara...hara..." voluntarily. '*My lord, the omniscient lord, please save my Ila*' I gave out a sharp yell.

It was then the change was slowing happening- Sudyumna was slowly changing into a woman, as Ila.

'*Oh, if calculated, this is the tenth month when the child is born. But if calculated as per the months she was cursed to change her gender, it is the day male Sudyumna will change into female Ila*'. My happiness knew no bounds. '*My Ila is going to give birth to my baby. O! God, My lord...*" I kept praying.

The child was born.

'*My lord, Thank you for showing me mercy. Thank you for saving my Ila and my baby.*' I kissed my baby out of ecstasy. Ila opened her eyes slowly, regained her consciousness. The baby cried. I smiled at her first sound of cry. '*The first king of the Lunar Dynasty, Pururuwas has thus taken birth on this universe. The first king of royal Kshatriya clan Pururuwas is crying here as a baby. All the problems of Ila must disappear henceforth. As her parent wished she should become a man permanently as Sudyumna. It is all possible only with the benevolence of God almighty.*'

"Om...Nama shivaya...Om Nama shivaya" I kept chanting as a mark of my gratitude.

Ended

About the Author

Alagarsamy Sakthivel, a citizen of Singapore, was born in Dindigul, Tamil Nadu, India. He completed his degree in Electronics from Alagappa Chettiar Government Engineering College in Karaikudi, Tamil Nadu. He did his post-graduation degree in software manufacturing from Singapore's Nanyang Technical University. He has a Master degree in Computer Application from Madras University, Tamil nadu.

He has been actively involved in writing on third gender and is presently working in Singapore. He has authored five books.

About the Translator

Saravanan Karmegam is hailing from Thiruppalaikudi, a coastal village in Ramanathapuram district, Tamil Nadu, India. He is an alumnus of Thiagarajar College- Madurai, English and Foreign Languages University (EFLU) - Hyderabad and Jawaharlal Nehru University (JNU) - New Delhi. He had served in Central Reserve Police Force (CRPF), India's biggest police organisation as Deputy Commandant. Presently he is working as a Deputy General Manager in one of the Reserve Bank of India subsidiary companies in Mysore, Karnataka, India.

Out of sheer passion towards translation, he has been actively involved with translating Tamil literary works into English. He is a regular contributor to Indian Literature, a bi-monthly magazine of Sahitya Akademi, New Delhi, India. His English translations are accessible at www.saravananpages.in.

www.ingramcontent.com/pod-product-compliance
Lightning Source LLC
LaVergne TN
LVHW041033150826
845672LV00001B/293

* 9 7 9 8 8 9 5 8 8 9 9 3 0 *